The Legacy

James Gilbert

• Chicago •

The Legacy

James Gilbert

Published by
Joshua Tree Publishing
• Chicago •
JoshuaTreePublishing.com

13-Digit ISBN Print: 978-1-956823-21-9
13-Digit ISBN eBook: 978-1-956823-30-1

Disclaimer:

This is a work of fiction. Names, characters, places, and incidents are the product of the author's imagination or have been used fictitiously. Any resemblance to actual persons, living or dead, events, locales or organizations is entirely coincidental.

Printed in the United States of America

Dedication

For Jonathan Auerbach,
from the beginning

Chapter 1

Adam Chauncey leaned back, balancing his feet atop his desk, and faced the entrance to his office. A dim light managed to seep through the opaque glass in the top half of the door, just bright enough that he could see the shadow of someone approaching from the other side. He had learned to judge the shapes: the shared secretary of all the juniors despite her changing hairstyles, the occasional partner who stopped by to hand off some assignment, or the cleaning person who pushed a large janitor cart with its round belly basket and stick figures of mops and brooms. But there was no window overlooking the river yet, if ever, and no name on his anonymous door.

He reminded himself that he needed to finish the research for a contract he'd been assigned the day before, but that could wait.

Instead, he recalled the lame saying that needled him in moments like this: that a paralegal could just dream of a partnership somewhere, and an associate might hope for one. Probably not much difference other than hope between the two, he thought, if you considered the similar work assignments and salaries. And about salaries, well, those were a closely guarded secret. No doubt to inspire competition and jealousy among the junior cohort.

He swung his feet down and moved the mouse around, lighting up his desktop. The background picture sprang up: a lone gray wolf with a trail of paw prints tracing across the top of a mountainous snowbank. And today's date—April 12. He paused before typing in his password. There was something about that particular day that jarred his memory. And then he recalled that it was almost exactly a year since Bill Evans, one of the senior partners of Smithson and Dwyer, had invited him to lunch at the Metropolitan Club just a few blocks down on West Wacker Drive. As far as he knew, most of the partners had a membership there, but it was expensive, way too expensive, for him yet. And he wondered if he even wanted to join an organization that described itself as the "gathering point for elevating personal and professional success." The club did, of course, have a magnificent view of the city and was renowned as a place where promises could be made and deals hatched in the muffled elegance of linen tablecloths and heavy silverware. But if nothing else, the monthly dues were high enough that he'd have to decide on paying them or his rent—so for the time being, that wasn't much of a choice.

He had been puzzled by this sudden attention from a higher up, from the "Tower," as all the juniors called the partners' elegant suite of offices. He had been pretty confident it wouldn't be a reprimand or criticism of his work. That was the job of the HR office, manned by Rachael Underwood (known to all the juniors as Rabid Underhand) and a woman of severe aspect, limited affability, and very few words. No, he realized that it had to be something good, although the request, when it finally came just before dessert, was certainly an odd and unexpected one.

After a meager lunch of soup and salad (Adam had ordered the same dishes as his host even though it was an elaborate and tempting menu) and a desultory conversation in which he had affirmed that, yes, he found his work stimulating (not entirely true); that he was single with an out-of-town ex-girlfriend (nothing serious there and probably over); that he loved Chicago (at least those parts of the city he knew); and that his mother was alive and thriving (exactly 332 miles away) down in Southern Illinois.

"I hope you're enjoying yourself here, young man," Bill Evans began as they waited for their coffee to be served. "Just look around you. This is a great club. Top of the competition. Nothing quite like it in the city. You ought to think about joining. Would be perfect for an ambitious lawyer making his way up."

"Thank you, sir," Adam said. "I agree. It's a terrific place."

"You probably guessed that I have something to ask you," Evans continued after the briefest pause. "It's not complicated at all, and I suspect you won't ever be called upon to act. So let's call it a kind of stop-gap favor."

"Of course, Bill, anything," he said, intentionally emphasizing his partner's first name, which still seemed inappropriately familiar to say.

"And no need for you to know any of the details," Evans continued. "But I want to put you down as co-executor of a will, as an alternative trustee. Pretty much standard nowadays. Most wills of any substance have joint trustees. You'll need to sign some papers, of course, but I can't imagine you'll be called upon to act. You see, I'll be the actual executor when the time comes. But I want to make sure there's some sort of back-up just in case. I'm sure you're aware that it gets complicated if a single executor is incapacitated for some reason. In that case, the court would usually appoint one of the heirs or siblings if there are any remaining. But that can lead to all sorts of squabbles, and in this instance, that's almost inevitable because it's a rather large fortune. Tends to bring out the sharks."

"I'll be happy to sign on," Adam said. "But can I ask who the will-maker is?"

"I don't believe that's necessary for you to know in this case. He's a very private person. I just need your signature."

"More than happy to agree," Adam said, although he wondered about the secrecy and if this was really standard or normal. He didn't have much experience with wills yet, but there was clearly something odd about this—several things, in fact. At that moment, he had been the most junior associate in the firm, and the ink on his diploma had scarcely dried. Did that have something to do with the request? And he wondered why the identity of the person had to be kept quiet—if that meant anything. Seemed as if it did. Of course, he was sure it would all be above board. The firm was steeped in tradition and respectability, but he couldn't help suspecting that something was odd. And then there was the merest suggestion that Evans was dangling a promotion—and a future place at the club—in front of him. He hoped that's all it was. But maybe this was just standard practice, and his eager imagination (as usual) was skipping two rungs up the ladder.

Bill had smiled and reached his hand across the table, and Adam had clutched it to seal the agreement.

Actually, as he sat remembering, it was exactly one year ago. But if this was a mystery, he had almost entirely forgotten it. He wasn't sure what made him think of it at that moment. The date, of course. Or maybe the screenshot of the wolf on his computer?

He had to admit he was never very good at premonitions. Most of his hunches turned out to be false and led to nowhere, like the time he had imagined himself strolling into the Sterling Library at Yale, fresh from his first undergraduate pre-law course, and passing under its high gloomy gothic arches into the cathedral interior, shimmering with soft, filtered light. It had been so real, although he knew now that it was only a false memory. At that time, it had seemed such a precise prediction and vision, almost material. He could almost feel the smooth paving stones under his feet and the exquisite silence of the great entrance hall. But, of course, it hadn't happened; his application had been rejected. He had graduated instead from Southern Illinois University in Carbondale, then on to the mid-level law school at Illinois at Champaign-Urbana halfway up the state, and finally to Chicago, where he had the unexpected and surprising good fortune to apply just at the right moment for a position at Smithson and Dwyer. At least that's what the interviewer told him at the time.

And then, the hasty prediction he imagined after his lunch with Bill Evans had been a quick rise up the ranks of the firm, taking on more and more responsibility, and further lunches and hints about an early partnership. But, so far, that, too, had proved a way-off-the-mark forecast. The tasks he was assigned were scarcely better than the grunt work piled on the paralegals who toiled in the open-plan pen on the bottom floor (ominously) close to the HR office. And, more surprising, on the rare occasion when he passed him in the hallway, Bill Evans didn't seem to recognize him, just giving him a stranger's empty smile. Lucky for both of them to be spared the chance encounter in the men's room because even the lavatories at Smithson and Dwyer were hierarchical, with the partner commodes located somewhere in the upper reaches of the top floor and requiring a special code to enter.

Just now, as he recalled the lunch meeting and the partner's request, Adam wondered if being co-executor might have been some sort of setup. Maybe he was chosen not for a rapid rise in the firm—their tousled-haired prodigy. Maybe he was chosen because he was new, inexperienced, and—he had to admit—pretty naïve. He had given his signature without question, eager to help out if needed, whatever that entailed, because, in his enthusiasm, he hoped it meant something. But instead, he had been dismissed back into the obscurity and anonymity of the lower reaches of the firm. So it was a puzzle even if—as usual—he was probably overthinking it.

True enough, a year toiling in the bottom ranks of a distinguished Chicago law office wasn't exactly the end of the world, but he had hoped for something better. He was aware, certainly, that not everyone would be handed the complicated and exciting problems that he had debated in his case law classes. In fact, when he first contemplated a legal degree and scrolled through the course offerings, he quickly realized that much of his profession was a slog in the muddy waters of contracts and administration— nothing like the adventures of lone protagonists in disheveled suits and dicey reputations that novelists and television series depicted. He had often thought of their stories as modern Westerns and the last hold-out of American individualism. And perhaps that's what first attracted him. But the reality, even more than he anticipated, was exactly the opposite. He was just a small player in a very large bureaucracy of advantage-seeking and cutting corners.

There was one thing he hadn't even imagined, however. He knew that the partners lived mostly in the northern suburbs, up on the bluffs that rose above the upper reaches of Lake Michigan. And he suspected that this was a tight-knit social group with a high price of admission and family privileges. Nonetheless, he was surprised when one of Dwyer's nephews, newly graduated from some law school in Florida that no one had ever heard of, joined the firm and snared an office on the upper floor with a window overlooking the Chicago River. And their initial introduction hadn't gone all that well, either. Everett Dwyer (E for short) was introduced to the other juniors and paralegals at one of their monthly get-togethers. After shaking hands, E looked over Adam's shoulder and mumbled something about an important person he spotted and fled. Later, as he circulated around the room, Adam caught snatches of his conversation: words like *yacht*, *cruise*, something about Nassau, and a whole sentence declaring that he was temporarily "crashing" with his uncle in the lakefront estate with a large stone house that Adam learned even had an elevator. He could foresee a bright future for this new junior and a quick ride up to the top ranks to partner. Goes to show you that pedigree counted in this best of show!

The next afternoon after that gathering, Sally Warren, one of the paralegals that he often worked with, stopped by and collapsed wearily into the client's chair opposite Adam's desk.

"That was a long day yesterday . . . and boring, wouldn't you say?" She paused to brush a wisp of blonde hair out of her eyes. "So what did you think of him?" she continued.

"Who? Oh, you mean E? Didn't really get a chance to talk to him much."

"Cut to the front of the line, I'd say."

"I guess you'd have to admit that he has a few advantages to take advantage of, yes."

"You're too kind, Adam. Much too forgiving, but I guess that's your country background or something. But I mean, what's all the catechism about merit and hard work that pays off when we're really just putting in all this effort to make the uppers look good? And now—"

"He seemed nice enough, inoffensive."

"I don't judge a bottle by its shape, Adam. Only what's inside. Speaking of which, I've decided to accept your standing invitation for a drink after work today."

"Fine," Adam said, a bit surprised but delighted at her abruptness: "I was about to leave. Just give me a second."

"Well, don't do anything special for me," she said, straightening in her chair and uncrossing her legs.

"That's what I like about you, Sally. Always the last word."

"You bet," she said, laughing. "Come on then, Junior. That place you mentioned?"

Bundled against the cold wind blowing off the lake, they walked down to the Elephant and Castle on West Adams. Adam hooked his arm for Sally to grasp as they made their way toward the pub, but she stuffed her hands in her pockets. The pub was located just far enough away that in this weather, they probably didn't risk meeting any of the other juniors and certainly not the partners, who preferred their cocktail hour at one or the other of their clubs.

Adam hadn't bothered to sort out his feelings about Sally yet. In fact, he thought if he did, it might create some sort of problem between them. Sure, she was very attractive, blunt, and assertive, and he admired that. A bit older than him, blonde, and dressed in a dark suit this afternoon. Once, he had thought she was too shy to talk about herself, but he decided it was just caution—a shield, like her sarcasm. In fact, he really didn't know much about her, just that she had graduated top of her class from a good school and came from one of the Carolinas. Whether she had a boyfriend or girlfriend or any kind of lover, he didn't know. Just that she was a pleasure to be around, and his life was currently running on empty in that regard. And anyway, he thought he had a sort of commitment elsewhere. Not that he was ready for a commitment.

"Table or bar?" he asked when they entered the warm, semi-dark establishment.

"Bar, for sure," she said, slinging off her coat and walking over to edge onto a stool at the middle of a long gleaming wooden counter.

"Fine with me," he said, joining her and nodding to the barista, who had just looked their way and was approaching.

"You know, I've always wanted to try that beer on the menu: Flying Dog Raging Bitch," she said, "Always wondered about that name. If it's actually for real."

"I didn't think the meeting yesterday was that bad!"

"Guess you're right. So I'll just have a Blue Moon on tap," she said. "I can always try the Bitch later."

"Same for me," he told the waiter.

"Not very original of you."

"I'm trying to husband my imagination."

"Oh yeah," she said. "Have you got a problem?"

"Not really. Nothing I want to discuss anyway."

"You know, Adam, that's just like you. You lay down a hint and then walk away from it like you just did something you're ashamed of."

"I guess you know me too well," he said as the waiter flipped two coasters on the bar in front of them and then placed their glasses on top.

"I'm not sure I know you at all."

"Likewise. Should I make a tab?" he asked.

"Sure," Sally called to the barista. "Adam is the name."

They both took a sip of their beers.

"You know what I like about this place? They serve drinks slightly warm, the way they do in an English pub," Adam said. "Not frozen, so you can actually taste it."

"Are you changing the subject, or is that just a long detour?"

"A feint to the right, then a tuck to the left. You know the technique. But no, I was just thinking today about Bill Evans. You remember, I told you about how friendly he had been last year about the will I signed as the second executor and then how he really cut me off with no explanation after that as if I had done something wrong or maybe become a nonperson. Doesn't seem to recognize me anymore."

"Could be he was embarrassed . . . or more likely, forgetful," she added.

"Whatever, it's still a puzzle," he said, taking a mouthful of beer and then pinching the froth from his lips with his forefinger and thumb.

"One piece of gossip you might not have heard. It might explain things," she said.

"Yeah?"

"Rumor has it he's sick or ready to retire, but in any case, absent from the office a lot recently."

"I hadn't heard that. Somehow, the echoes from the second floor don't penetrate the concrete as far down as my basement cubby hole."

"Well, if you'd pay attention, you'd learn a lot more," she said, tilting her glass in a mock salute toward him.

"Cheers," she said.

"Cheers."

After another round of drinks, Sally suddenly announced that she was ready to leave, and without waiting for him to object, she shrugged on her coat and slipped off the bar stool.

"We can share an Uber if you want. I'll let you off first. Near North Side, isn't it?" she said.

"Sure," he replied, trying to relax a frown of disappointment. If the trip had been the other way round, with his destination last, he thought he might invite her in for the evening. He had often imagined something like that, but every time there was the slightest chance, she became mysterious about where she lived or found some excuse to leave early and on her own. It wasn't as if he was in hot pursuit of an office romance. And he feared that, with Sally, it would never be anything more than comfortable sex and the kind of intimacy that felt great at the time but left no void or hunger that could trouble you the next day with frustration or regrets. He was sure she understood this, too, but perhaps, he thought that wouldn't be enough for her. And he was supposed to have a girlfriend who had taken a job with a law firm in Des Moines. But he understood from their agreed-upon silence and emails unsent that it wasn't just the distance between them that was keeping them apart.

At least one good thing had come from the evening with Sally, however. He now had a reason to inquire about Bill Evans and his strange behavior. And he also understood that tonight was no night for romance. His apartment was a mess, and his unmade bed was an uninviting jumble of sheets. Anything so spur of the moment would be embarrassing, and he would be all apologies. No way to begin even the most casual relationship.

The next morning, he sat in his office, staring at a file that had appeared like magic, as they often did, on his desk during the night or dawn hours. The Brief Gremlin, he thought, had struck again, and he wondered if any of the other juniors had received a work packet that morning. It was an unspoken understanding among the associates to keep quiet about the work the partners shoveled into the basement of the firm. No one ever wanted to admit to being under- or overworked with the consequence that everyone said they were "busy," even if it meant you'd been staring at your cell phone all hours or the opposite: staying late every night for a month and only drinking a jigger or two of scotch for dinner. Every junior at the firm pretty much kept their assignments in their own private silo. Of course, he had told Sally about being the joint executor on that anonymous will, but that was hardly significant.

He opened the folder and read the cover letter from the secretary to one of the partners. Nothing important or worthy of five-hundred-dollar-an-hour attention from upstairs. And certainly no rush, either, he decided, and pushed it aside. He hesitated for a moment and then stood up, grabbing his jacket and pulling his tie knot close to his neck as he walked out of his office to the bank of elevators. Inside he punched "2" and waited as the doors slid closed, enveloping him in the wood-paneled silence of second-floor luxury. For clients, this elevator ride would be their first encounter with the firm, but for him, it was a reminder of his status down in the cement-block underworld.

Almost immediately, muted chimes signaled the door opening, and he stepped out into the main reception area onto the thick green carpet. He stepped immediately to the left, nodding to the young man behind the reception desk, and walked into a hallway that led toward the end to a large room where several secretaries sat in front of computer terminals. When he entered, he could hear the faint, rhythmic exhale of the copy machine. He knew only one of the persons (not just women) who worked here. A diversity mandate had introduced a couple of young men into the pool, and they generally avoided him. But his friend, Lizbeth Lowry, looked up at him, however, as if she expected a visit.

"Well, Adam," she said, getting up from her chair. "What brings you up to heaven?"

"It wasn't for the rapture yet," he laughed.

"You're welcome, nonetheless. How have you been? Busy?"

"I'm great," he said. And then paused. "I don't suppose I could buy you a free coffee in the lounge?"

"Of course you can. Just let me finish this paragraph. I'll meet you outside."

He stepped away from her desk and turned back down the hall and entered the lounge area. There were several dark leather chairs placed for casual conversation around a large, low table. A couple of pristine issues of the *Chicago Law Journal* lay scattered around the top. On one side was a small, discreet kitchen area with a large coffee machine, a sink, and a tray of porcelain cups and saucers next to a cardboard box dispenser of coffee pouches.

When Liz entered the lounge, Adam thought he could detect, as he always did around her, a slight change in the atmosphere. He had once asked her if she wore a perfume called Expectation.

"You're almost right," she had replied, laughing. "But the actual name is Experience."

Today, as always, she was dressed in black, with the white collar of a blouse that emerged from the sweater she was wearing. She was the kind of woman with a deep voice that made you think of cigarettes and brandy and a laugh that lodged in her throat. But he knew she never smoked or rarely drank. Just the kind of old-fashioned sophistication for a leading lady in a film noir—but without the platinum-blonde hair . . . or the danger. In fact, her hair was dark with facets of auburn. He couldn't remember how he had first met her, but it was one of those friendships that had seemed inevitable.

"I'll bet you want something, Adam. And don't worry about getting me any coffee. I'm fine. You get some if you want. And then just go ahead and ask."

"Well," he said after the machine spat out a murky liquid into his cup. "Why don't we sit down?"

"Sure, but I haven't got much time this morning. So shoot."

"I'm curious about something I heard—just a rumor actually," he began. "It's about one of the partners—Bill Evans. I heard that he is frequently absent from the office. Sick maybe or planning to retire . . . easing his way out."

"What makes you ask?"

"If you don't mind, I'd rather not say. But if you could tell me . . ."

"Well, now, if you're going to be mysterious. I wasn't aware you knew him personally. So I'll only tell you if you promise you'll let me in on the secret eventually."

"Promise. But I'll only tell you now that, yes, he and I've run into each other on occasion."

"All right. It's only palace gossip, but apparently, there are some signs of early Alzheimer's. Or maybe just an occasional dropped memory. Nothing right now that he can't manage, but I suppose the other partners will want him to retire soon."

"That's too bad."

"Might be, and what I just told you doesn't leave this lounge—ever. And, of course, I didn't tell you. 'Plausible deniability' as the politicians say. I'll certainly claim I didn't say a word."

"No need to worry. It's not important. I just—"

"Yes?"

"Nothing. Nothing at all."

"So," she said, getting up. "I ought to get back. And you owe me a real coffee sometime. This stuff tastes like paint thinner."

"It's a deal. And thanks, Liz. I won't say a word."

"We'll see," she said as she glided out the door. "We'll see, won't we?" she added, turning to glance back.

Adam remained for a minute more, staring at his coffee. He wasn't sure what had prompted his errand to confirm the rumors about Bill Evans. If he was truly incapacitated, that might explain why he received a blank stare whenever their paths crossed. But there might be one unexpected consequence: he'd have to be executor of that mysterious will if it came to it. That is until they appointed a new executor if they were going to. Only it wasn't really so mysterious. He just hadn't been allowed to see the person's name, and right now, that didn't matter much.

He stood up and mumbled, "Back to lower depths."

Chapter 2

pringtime in Chicago was often nothing more than a vague hint unless you looked carefully for the signs, like a few shivering daffodils and crocuses in pots pushed out onto the sidewalk in front of a florist shop. Or you might realize that the shadows cast by the elevated tracks in the Loop were shorter, and a bit more sunlight splashed onto the streets beneath. And now, when the wind blew off the lake, it seemed exhausted and out of breath as the cold fronts weakened and expended their energy over Wisconsin. You might also notice muffled faces beginning to emerge from wrappings of scarves and hoods as if the milder weather was peeling off the linen from features long mummified against the chill. The few remaining snow and ice patches turned black with soot and dust would be melted away, leaving gritty wet splotches on the sidewalks. If you looked east through the dark tunnels framed by the blocks of office buildings, you might glimpse patches of green that began to appear in the parks along Michigan Avenue. But spring, Adam thought as he walked up along the river toward Smithson and Dwyer, was always a tentative and fragile thing that emerged cautiously from its winter lair. And then suddenly, it would be summer: sweaty, humid, violent summer.

Once inside the building and walking along the corridor to his office, he could see lights in several of the other offices (the early-hour juniors), and he heard the indistinct noise of conversations emerging through the open door to the paralegal chamber as he passed by. For some reason, when he opened his office this morning, the room that sprang into the light that he switched on looked even smaller and shabbier than he remembered it. Inevitably, his eyes focused first on the diploma he had reluctantly fastened to the wall—a requirement of the firm. And then he looked at the desk and the chair behind it, where he would spend most of the day, reading, scribbling notes on a yellow legal pad, and then transferring his work to the computer that sat on an extension that made a right angle to the desk. He resisted the temptation to turn around and walk out.

As he hung up his coat, he wondered what it was today that had put him in such a sour mood. Spring, however tentative, was supposed to fill you with optimism and promise, yet he felt troubled and nervous. He had been with the firm for little over a year, and he certainly couldn't complain. His salary was more than adequate, and the assignments weren't difficult, even if they often seemed like piecework. But this morning, he felt that he wasn't going anywhere, just polishing his shoes for a dance without a partner. He was pretty sure he knew the problem: it was boredom. He was bored with detail and bored with the insignificant legal matters that came his way. But what had he expected then? He asked himself. To make partner in his first year? To ascend to the Tower and earn a key to a better bathroom and spend two martini lunches with clients at some expensive club he had been privileged to join?

As he settled into his chair, he had the recurring thought that perhaps he lacked ambition, the yearning for advancement that transformed all the menial tasks he would be assigned into the small steps upward that imaginary staircase to success. Perhaps, he thought, ambition was a way to kid yourself into performing a job that, if you mulled it over too long, you might really detest. Ambition, he thought—that infinitely capacious word! It was what provided the energy that allowed the firm to function. Ambition maintained the hierarchy itself and made every lowly position tolerable. It abbreviated time. Ambition was the sentence that began: "If I just . . ." Of course, there was the promise of a happy ending. But he wondered: was he somehow deficient in that simple quality that seemed to motivate everyone else in this profession?

Reluctantly, he opened his computer, glanced at the schedule for the day, and then scrolled down to the brief that one of the partners had asked him to complete. It was something new for him—a complicated property dispute. He decided to ask Sally, who had more experience with such cases, if he was pursuing the correct angle. And to be honest, he had another reason to ask her.

Picking up his yellow pad and a couple of pens, he stepped out into the corridor and walked down to the paralegal's office. As always, the door was slightly ajar, and he could see her sitting at her desk off toward the left of the room.

"Mind if I consult for a minute?" he said, approaching her.

And then he realized that she was on the telephone. When she saw who it was, she gestured for him to sit next to her.

After a minute or two, in which her end of the conversation was a string of uh-huhs and nods, she hung up and said, "Caught me. Brother called from Raleigh."

"Any problem?"

"Do you have any siblings, Adam? If you did, you wouldn't ask."

"Not that I do, but I won't ask."

"I take it this isn't a social call," she said, gesturing to the yellow pad he had placed on his lap.

"It is, and it isn't," he said. "I'm just wondering if you'd look at these notes I've made. Just to let me know if I'm on the right track."

She looked slightly disappointed.

"And then I'd like to buy you a drink today after work. Elephant and Castle?"

"Not there today, perhaps. How about the South Branch instead? We can sit outside if it's not too cold. Maybe I'm rushing spring a bit, but I wouldn't mind trying. And sure, I'll take a look at what you've done. Hand it over."

"Perfect," Adam said. He stood up and gave Sally his notes. "You're a pal," he said as he turned to leave. He thought he heard her mumble something, but he continued out the door.

When he got back to his office, he continued to work on the brief, but after a couple of hours, he suddenly stopped and looked up. It occurred to him that he had sounded crass with Sally—made it seem like this was some kind of transaction. "You help me out, and the payoff will be that I'll buy you a drink." In fact, when he thought about it, it was the other way around. His request had been an excuse to see her, and what he really wanted was the payoff: a casual date. For some reason, in the last few months, he had kept to himself. But now, he thought, he was really wanting to see more of her. Maybe it was spring.

It was chilly sitting out on the patio of the restaurant, but the view of the Chicago River and the city in the fading light of the late afternoon was exhilarating. It was one of the things he liked best about the city: its absolutely level terrain and a straight-line horizon broken up by the shimmering tall buildings, where, on the surface of one after the other, lighted windows would soon appear like stars emerging from the darkening dusk. Two cinnamon hot tequila toddies sat on the table in front of them—a drink suggested by the waiter as the special of the afternoon.

"I usually don't like pretentious drinks like this," Sally said as she picked up her glass. "But today, it seems a perfect fit."

"For sure," he said.

She looked carefully at him, and then her face broke out in amusement.

"So serious, Adam? What's up? You usually don't ask me out without a reason."

"Damn, Sally. You're reason enough. Don't sell yourself short," he said. "But actually, there is something."

"I thought so. So shoot. But just don't let it be about the firm. I'm in no mood this afternoon for office gossip."

"It is, and it isn't," he said. "Maybe it's the change of seasons, or maybe it's something else, but I'm thinking of quitting. Maybe go into practice for myself."

"Ha!" she laughed. "You've been reading too many John Grisham novels. You think that a trial lawyer is some kind of hero? Like an undercover detective? A middle-class superhero in a tattered suit and driving an old Chevy around the New Orleans bayous? Dragging into court between binges? Getting some poor soul off the hook, really? You're wanting that?"

"But what's the alternative? Working in a firm, making partner, moving to Winnetka, a house by the lake, golf every Sunday, trophy wife, martinis with the partners?"

"What's so bad about that? And if you're at the top, you get to choose the cases you work on. Challenge yourself as much as you want."

"Or as little."

"Christ, Adam. You're really cynical today."

"Maybe I'm just being realistic."

She paused and took another sip of her drink and shook her head. "The trouble with a hot toddy is that it cools off. Now listen, Adam. That word *realistic*, isn't that just another way of saying *pessimistic*? Whenever someone says *realistic* to me, I expect—and I usually get—a laundry list of all the awful things that they can think of."

He looked at her face, slightly flushed from the cold and illuminated in the dying sunlight. She had never appeared to him as lovely, but maybe it wasn't how she looked at all but the attraction he felt in her words. Sensible, he thought, could fool you into thinking beautiful.

"I suppose you're right. And I will admit that there's at least a small pleasure in figuring out a winning argument or writing the perfect clause in a contract. Tying a knot that can't be untied. I suppose I should take satisfaction in that. It's just that—"

"Don't," she interrupted. "Don't spoil everything with that thought. And please stop being realistic!"

She pulled up the left sleeve of her jacket and glanced at her watch.

"I'd better be leaving now," she said. "Thanks for the drink. I'll see you tomorrow. And stop thinking of quitting. Something interesting is bound to come along."

She stood up, reached across the table, and punched him lightly on the shoulder, and then she left.

As he watched her make her way back into the tavern and then disappear in the obscurity of its dim lighting, he wondered why he hadn't asked her to stay, to have dinner later. But every time such a moment occurred—when he might do so—she slipped away. Next time, he vowed, it would be a real date. Maybe that's what was bothering him. And he had entirely forgotten to thank her for her notes on the contract dispute.

The next morning was back to winter, with frozen pellets of sleet bouncing on a cold wind and skittering onto the sidewalk. Low gray clouds shrouded the lake and cut off the tops of the downtown skyscrapers. Spring was playing its usual game of "catch me if you can," but he wasn't in the mood to join in. The night before, he had drunk too many scotches and dined on frozen pizza, and the two fought to a dyspeptic draw in his stomach, leaving him with a headache and a queasy feeling. He didn't even think of breakfast.

He entered his office, hung up his scarf and winter coat, and stood for a reluctant minute before he walked around his desk. When he sat down, he noticed a post-it clinging to his computer screen. Picking it up, he read: "Call Mr. Dwyer's office ASAP."

It wasn't often that he received messages from the upper floor with any urgency, although it was normal to receive an email or find a brief laid on his desk. It certainly couldn't be bad news, he thought, because he was confident that his work was perfectly adequate, even good sometimes. Anyway, the partners rarely interfered with the duties they assigned to HR. So he picked up the phone and called upstairs.

The secretary answered.

"It's Adam Chauncey calling for Mr. Dwyer. I have a message to get in touch."

"Yes, Mr. Chauncey. Mr. Dwyer would like to see you this morning. Could you be in his office around ten?"

From her tone, he understood this wasn't a question, and because she didn't allow any uncertainty in her voice to rise at the end of the sentence, it sounded more like a command.

"Certainly. I'll be there."

"We expect you then," she said and hung up.

Adam leaned back in his chair, hands locked behind his head, puzzled about the summons and the brusque way the secretary had spoken to him. Perhaps she might be relaying something unpleasant, he thought, and transmitting the dissatisfaction of her superior. Or maybe he was imagining some unpleasant suggestion conveyed in her voice. He had speculated, on occasion, that a messenger could be like a ventriloquist suggesting the real intent of the message sender, someone to relay something unspoken but apparent by a subtle inflection or tone. But in this case, he decided that the secretary was just being perfunctory and businesslike. It was probably his sour disposition this morning distorting his anticipation. He needed to stop analyzing and wait for the meeting.

A few minutes before 10:00 a.m., he left the office and stood in front of the elevator. Although it rose only one floor, the world was different when he emerged onto the thick royal-green carpet into the main lobby. A young man sat at a reception desk adjacent to the corridor that led to the partners' offices. He gave Adam an off-handed glance and then looked down at something he seemed to be studying.

"You are Mr. Chauncey?" he asked without looking up.

Adam nodded.

"Please wait. Mr. Dwyer is busy at the moment. Just take a seat, and I'll let you know when he can see you."

For some reason, the man's unfriendly attitude irked him, and he was about to say something caustic when he thought, no, he's probably just glued to Facebook on his cell phone and bored beyond intolerable. After all, what was his job like running a triage for clients?

He sat down on an upholstered leather chair next to a low table and waited.

After about a half hour, the young man looked his way and said quietly, "Mr. Dwyer will see you now."

Adam got up and walked quickly across the room and down the corridor. He stopped in front of the door with Dwyer's name embossed in gold lettering on a frosted panel. Knocking firmly, he stepped inside.

The room he entered was, in fact, the antechamber to Dwyer's office, and the secretary who had called him—he assumed it was her—was stationed at a desk on one side. She looked up from her computer and waved a hand at him.

"Just go on in. Mr. Chauncey, is it? And please don't bang on the door. He doesn't like that."

He nodded, walked over to the door, and pushed it open.

Dwyer was sitting behind an immense mahogany desk with edge pillars carved to look like long-legged cranes. All along the walls, there were color prints of hunting scenes: spotted dogs pointing at unseen quail hiding in the brush, men dressed in elegant camouflage gear shouldering rifles, and one striking portrait of a hunter holding a clutch of limp pheasants with their luminous blue, green, and gold throat feathers vivid (at least in the painter's mind) even in death.

"You wanted to see me, Mr. Dwyer," Adam said.

"Indeed, Chauncey, sit down. Over there," he said, pointing. "I'll join you in a second." He picked up a file, stood, and walked over to the conference table just as Adam remained standing behind one of the chairs.

"Sit down, sit down," Dwyer ordered. Adam thought he could see impatience and exasperation in the older man's face.

When they were both seated, Dwyer slid the file across the polished surface.

"You'll be familiar with this, I understand," he said.

Adam opened it up and saw that it was a will, and he immediately realized what it was, and he didn't have to guess why he was there.

"This is really an unfortunate situation," Dwyer began. "I'm not entirely sure why Bill had you sign on as a co-executor—someone so completely inexperienced. But who knows? He had his reasons, I imagine." He fell silent as if waiting for Adam to say something. "Well, be that as it may," he resumed suddenly, "it looks like you're going to be the lead executor of this will. We could always appoint another executor, but I think I'd like to give you a chance. I've heard some good things about your work."

"Thank you, sir."

"Here's the problem," he continued. "Bill's somewhat indisposed these days. I suspect you've heard rumors down in the basement. Gossip spreads around here like the plague. But anyway, he shouldn't fulfill his duty right now, and that leaves you. Have you read the will? Do you know who Percy Landsman is?"

"I haven't a clue," Adam replied. "I just agreed to what Mr. Evans asked, and I signed. Didn't read it. Admittedly, I was a bit puzzled at the time, but he didn't explain anything."

"So you don't know what the bequests are, I'm assuming, or any of the stipulations."

"No. I just signed to be co-executor in case . . ."

Dwyer sighed as if he was facing a task of heavy lifting. "Well," he began again, "The party in question, Mr. Percy Landsman, is now deceased, and you'll be tasked with executing the will. I have to warn you that there's a large fortune at stake. So I don't want any mistakes."

He paused, and Adam saw a funny look on his face before he said, "Damn Evans for putting an amateur in charge!"

"I'll do my best, sir," said Adam, trying to ignore what had just been said. "And I'll consult with you if I run into any problems. Unless you think I'm not up to it."

"You're damned right you'll consult. Me or Mr. Emsback. Probably the latter. He's our will and testament expert and drew up this document. And I can warn you that there may be a lot of junk on the road before you get to the end of it. There always is. Landsman was an odd character. But try to ignore that! Get one of the paralegals to do some of the leg work. And don't disappoint me. I'm taking a chance on you. Don't mess this up and make it complicated. Just be quick, get it done, and don't ask questions."

"Sir," Adam said.

"And one more thing. Bill had a power of attorney with the Harris Bank, but with the death, that's expired. But as executor, you'll have access to his account there, so if you incur any expenses in your duties, you'll have to apply to them. Don't come running to me or Emsback for everything despite what I just said. All the information you need is in the file."

"All right," Adam said. He was puzzled about expenses, even more about Dwyer's apparent haste, but he didn't ask.

"Well, that's all for now," Dwyer said. "Take this copy of the will. Study it and get moving. I'll have my secretary send you a version online also. But I always find it's easier to think about a case if I have a piece of paper in front of me. That's all for now," he said, standing up. "There's a good boy."

After his dismissal, Adam rode the elevator back down to his office, shut the door, cleared off his desk, and sat for a moment staring at the file the partner had given him—shoved at him would be more accurate. His gesture was more than a hint that he was happy to hand off this task to someone else, as if the file contained something unpleasant or impossible or maybe just something too detailed and beneath his dignity. But at the same time, he seemed to have some second thoughts about his decision. Whatever the case, it now belonged to Adam. He'd have to prove himself. But he still wondered.

As he sat, skimming through several pages, he confirmed that the prefatory statements had been carefully drawn. Skipping past what looked like several charitable bequests and their percentages of the estate, he found the short list of beneficiaries, their addresses, and in a separate document, the financial institutions where Evans retained his investments. Going back a second time, he noted that there were a few specific items granting large sums to several charities and only two specific beneficiaries. Based on a more careful accounting, he estimated that the deceased had been a very rich man, and that might well explain the very careful way the will was drawn. On the last page, he found his signature as well as that of Evans. But then there were two more sheets, including something that seemed quite odd to Adam. The first instructed the executors to send an explanatory letter to each of the two beneficiaries. And on the second was the very strange mention of some unknown family. He would have to worry about that later.

Adam understood his first task would be to compile and locate the financials of the estate and then try to anticipate any difficulties that might arise with such a large fortune at stake, let alone the tax implications. You couldn't cover every contingency, he thought, or worry about the most preposterous and unexpected claims that might develop when such large sums were involved. In his limited experience, families and friends could be driven crazy when it came to money—any amount of money! In fact, it seemed, the smaller, the more bitter the acrimony. It was always a question of perceived fairness when death defined degrees of affection in percentages.

Fortunately, the deceased had carefully listed his primary possessions, including the financial institutions holding his investments and the approximate value of his residence. But Adam anticipated hard work to get an accurate estimate before he could distribute anything. He'd have to have help. Of course, he intended to ask Sally. Not only was she efficient and canny, but it would be a great excuse to see more of her.

He smiled as he closed the file. Maybe it wouldn't be as bad as he thought. Maybe he shouldn't be suspicious of Dwyer. Whatever he knew, the man was probably only sharing his delight not to be involved in the busywork of probating a complicated will that required considerable work and little reward . . . except—

Chapter 3

For the next week or so, he and Sally worked through the financials of the will. She proved more than adept at locating the right person at the various investment houses and holding companies where Landsman had placed his money. Adam knew he would never have the patience to keep from shouting at the voice announcing a call would be recorded "for training purposes" or listen to the jingling music on endless hold. Both of them were impressed and then amazed as the tally mounted up, although still surprised by how widely he had dispersed his fortune.

"If I didn't know any better," Adam said one late morning as they sat in his office, "I'd say there's something odd about the way he spread out all those investments—like he was trying to hide something or didn't trust anyone. Maybe that's what Dwyer meant when he warned me."

"You don't know better," she replied.

"True enough. I don't know a damn thing about Landsman, except that he seems like a strange person. As if there are some things we don't know about him and aren't listed here."

"That's why you have me," she laughed. "Your very own para-detective!"

"Seriously, though," he said. "Maybe I should talk to the brother. I know he's the principal beneficiary. Get some idea about who this guy was. And maybe he can help me locate the other person named in the will. I know you've been working on it, but from what you say, that woman seems elusive. I haven't asked you yet today, but any more luck in locating her?"

"Still no," she answered, "I only have an old address, and it seems she's since left. At least no response from her and no forwarding address."

"Well, we really can't have a reading until we've found and notified everyone—and when we know an approximation of the funds at stake."

"I think that's a good idea," she said. "Let's talk to the brother. Find out who Percy Landsman really was in real life—and not just a paper trace. But maybe first you should talk to the partner who's listed as the first executor."

"I'm not sure. He's supposed to be ill. Maybe he won't remember. Or won't see us."

"Come on, Adam," she said. "What's the harm? And he might tell you something. After all, he's the first person of record."

"OK," Adam said. "I'll call upstairs and find out about him."

"And if you want, I'll certainly go with you. Flash my winning smile and then sit quietly, taking notes. Watch for telling facial cues."

Still looking at her, Adam picked up the phone and called the head secretary, who ran interference for the squad of partners.

As soon as she answered, he began: "This is Adam Chauncey speaking. I'm the executor instead of Bill Evans for the Percy Landsman will. I'm wondering if I might consult with Mr. Evans. There are a number of issues I'm not quite clear on. But I wasn't sure if it was appropriate. Can you help me out?"

Mrs. Purvis at the other end paused for a minute and then said, "I doubt it very much, young man. He's on sick leave."

Although he hadn't spoken to her often, Adam was well aware—from her reputation as front doorkeeper and appointment secretary for the second floor—that the first words she uttered were invariably negative. She had a reputation for maintaining a strict hierarchy and protecting the partners from pestering juniors. But he insisted anyway. "It's really rather important."

"All right. I'll consult with one of the partners. But I can't promise anything except that I'll let you know."

He hung up the phone and turned to Sally. "It's a no, and then a maybe."

"I'd say that's pretty good on the first try," she said. "By the way, I almost forgot. You'll want to see this. It's the obit from yesterday's *Tribune.*"

"Any other evidence you're withholding?" he laughed.

"Nothing of consequence."

She handed him a clipping, which read:

CHICAGO BUSINESSMAN DECEASED

Percy Landsman, a well-known businessman and philanthropist, passed away Monday evening after a long illness. Mr. Landsman was born in 1945 in Chicago and was the adopted son of Ralph and Ester Landsman. He attended Beloit College, where he was president of his senior class and an outstanding athlete in several sports. After college, he attended the University of Chicago School of Business and then made Chicago his home. While at the university, he married Emma Taylor (now deceased). The couple had one son who served in Vietnam and died in combat.

Mr. Landsman was the president of Landsman Investment House, and he was a major contributor to several cultural institutions in Chicago. He served on the board of directors of Cliff Dwellers Club and several corporations. He is survived by a brother, Eric Landsman, of Chicago.

"Not much information there and certainly nothing odd. He sounds like the typical business success."

"So, nothing suspicious except for the fact that it doesn't say anything."

"Yes, I see that. Doesn't help us fill in the outstanding details of the will. I wonder who he really was."

The phone interrupted what he was about to say, and he picked up the receiver. "Chauncey here."

"Mr. Chauncey. Mr. Dwyer has given a tentative OK to a short meeting with Mr. Evans. You'll have to call his home and set things up. His wife will make the decision, of course, and if she says no, you're not to contact either of them again. Is that understood? I'll text you the information."

"Agreed, and thank you very much," Adam said, putting down the receiver.

"Why does that woman always sound like she means 'no' even when she says 'yes'?"

"Something about covering her ass, I suppose. Can't really criticize her for ambiguity. So if things go wrong, it'll always be your fault."

Later that afternoon, Sally and Adam were driving up to Winnetka in her car—the more presentable of their two and a vehicle that she often parked in a downtown garage near the office. Despite the long winter, everything was budding green, and the expansive lawns were brilliant with forsythia and some red bush that neither of them could identify.

"I always think that these people up here pay to have better weather," Adam said. "Like you could buy a bright day and a brilliant sunset. Money doesn't grow on trees in Winnetka, but it sure helps the trees to grow."

"You're just bitter because you're not a partner yet," she said, slowing down to turn into the circular driveway of a very large, set-back stone house. "I'm sure this is the address. No numbers anywhere—I guess that would be too common—but this has got to be it from the description Mrs. Purvis gave us. I guess you're just supposed to know where you are, and if you don't, you certainly have no business being here."

She stopped slightly before the front door, and they got out and walked to the entrance.

The house itself was a rambling three-story limestone construction with what looked like a conservatory in the south wing. The middle was a large flat portion pierced by rows of windows. This was no doubt the main part of the house. And then, on the other wing was a large two-story extension that could be a ballroom or even a small theater. Or perhaps a library.

As they approached, the door opened, and a very handsome, elderly woman stopped halfway out. Everything about her was elegant: a tailored dark-green suit, perfectly dyed and coiffed blonde hair, and a smooth tanned face and arms that suggested winters in Palm Beach and expensive spa work.

"You must be from the firm. Mr. Chauncey, is it?" she said, ignoring Sally. "We're expecting you. Please come in. It's still so chilly out." She clutched her arms with an exaggerated shiver.

She retreated inside, and they followed her into a surprisingly elegant and spacious hallway, her heels clicking on the glistening white marble floor. A pair of half-moon staircases on either side spiraled up to a second-floor landing. And at the end of the central hallway, down a long corridor, was a large window that telescoped a distant view of gardens and a smudge of the cloudy afternoon.

Adam looked at Sally and raised his eyebrows as if he was surprised not to find a gloomy gallery with standing suits of armor and heraldry draped on the walls—but not this!

"I'm Mrs. Evans, Gertrude Evans," she said, stopping. "Now, before I take you in to see Bill, I want to caution you not to stay too long. In fact, I'll come in and interrupt you when I think it's been long enough. You're lucky today seems to be one of his better days so far. You may not notice anything, but please don't say anything to upset him."

Without waiting for a response, she turned again and led them along the hallway past a large living room and then turned down a corridor to the left.

"He's in the library," she said, knocking quietly on a door about halfway to the end and then entering.

"Your appointments from the firm are here, Bill. I've told them not to stay long. Can I get you anything?"

He was sitting in the middle of the room on a leather chair with a reading lamp hooked over his left shoulder and an open book in his lap.

The room itself had two levels, lined with books on three sides and a circular iron staircase that wound up to a catwalk around the upper level. One entire wall looked to be identically bound legal volumes. A large bay window looked out the back toward an expanse of lawn and then the distant gray line of Lake Michigan.

Evans stood up and shook hands with his visitors and pointed to a sofa opposite his chair.

"It's a bit early for a drink," he said, ignoring his wife. "But you could have tea or coffee if you want."

"Thanks so much," Sally said. "But we'll only take a minute or two of your time."

He looked at them intensely: "OK. You're Miss . . . ?"

"Sally Warren. I work in the paralegal department. And this is Adam Chauncey."

"Adam, yes, of course. Well, I suppose you've come about that Landsman will. Odd character. Sorry to dump that on you, but it's more out of caution than anything. Might risk a lawsuit if I remained the executor . . . claims of incapacitation. Not that I am, really. Just that my memory isn't always great these days. And there's a doctor's diagnosis. But I suppose you know about that. So how can I help you?"

Mrs. Evans listened carefully for a moment and then walked quietly out of the room, leaving the door slightly ajar. Her husband walked over and closed it and then turned back.

"Please sit down."

He resumed his place and then said, "OK. What do you want to know?"

"Thanks very much for helping us," Adam began. "Ms. Warren here is assisting with research on the financials. As you probably know,

Landsman's assets are rather complicated—strewn about—and we're not sure that we have located all of them yet. But I'd like to know a couple of things. First, what can you tell me about Percy Landsman? And also, do you have any information about the second beneficiary? We have the woman's social security number and an old address, but we've had trouble locating her so far. We don't even know if she's still alive. But anything you can tell us would help with probate. But most of all, there's that curious letter he included that mentions his birth family. I'm sure you know what I'm talking about."

"Letter? Oh yes, I remember now. I advised him not to include that. Terrible! Just inviting lawsuits and more complications. But sometimes, a client is pig-headed, can't let go, and wants to have the last word. You know, arrange the chairs after the music stops. Troublesome man."

"Anything you can tell us about him would help."

"Who?" Evans asked, looking at them curiously as if he didn't recognize them.

"Landsman. We're talking about his will."

"Oh, that, yes. Straightforward, I always say. Don't confuse things that'll drag you into court every time. Didn't they teach you that in law school, young man?"

"But it isn't straightforward, is it? And what about Landsman? What was he like? "

Evans looked puzzled for a minute, putting his hand to the side of his head. Finally, he replied, "Landsman. Yes. Well, I can't tell you much. I wasn't his personal lawyer, just advised about the will and agreed to be executor. My partner Frank Emsback actually wrote it. Anyway, Landsman told me that his wife was deceased, and I think no children . . ." He stopped mid-sentence and looked at Sally. "What did you say your name was, young lady?"

"Sally Warren. From the firm."

"The firm? Oh yes, Smithson and Dwyer. You know I've been a partner there for a long time. Just taking a short vacation right now. What else was it you wanted to know? Did I forget something?"

"We were asking you about Percy Landsman," Adam interrupted.

"Oh yes. Landsman. Quite a character. Father came up from somewhere on the South Side. Made quite a success. And young Percy, he was adopted, you know, but still made his way up to the top of Chicago business. Great philanthropist. Had a younger brother. Gave away lots of money. A bit strange-looking, he was. I always wondered about that. Never understand why exactly. Dark."

"Do you have any idea about his businesses . . . what he did?"

Evans paused. "Oh yes, you mean Landsman. No, aside from his investment company, I don't know much. Very secretive about his personal life, although he was one of those public figures you would always see at the opening of an art gallery or a new play. But I didn't know him that well. Rumor was that he played his cards close to his chest."

"Do you have any idea why he dispersed his fortune in the way he did? We've had no trouble finding his brother, but there's that woman we can't trace."

"What?"

"Landsman's bequests."

"Did I tell you what a public figure he was? Always at openings of galleries or some new play. But I didn't know him all that well. Met him a few times, but—" Adam looked at Sally, who had a strange look on her face.

Evans stood up abruptly. "Would you mind if I called my wife? Maybe she can help you out. She's on every charity and nonprofit board in the city." Saying that, he walked quickly out of the room and, after a minute or two, returned with Mrs. Evans.

"I thought you'd like to talk to these two nice people who've come to ask me some questions about the firm," he said, walking in behind her. "Maybe you can answer better. I'm sure you remember what it was like when we first came to Chicago. Chicago in the fifties! What a place! Everything stirring and so much opportunity then. You're both so young! But I don't think I'd advise you to go into corporate law now if that's what you're thinking. It's changed so much lately. Just endless litigation, contracts. You'll just be part of a bureaucracy and never your own boss. Of course, there's criminal law. But I don't know much about that. No, I'd try another profession. You're both so young."

"Sit down, Bill," Mrs. Evans ordered. "I'll see these two out."

She walked over to the door and opened it, guiding Sally and Adam with her eyes.

Once in the front hall, she said, "I'm sorry, but I had to interrupt. Once he starts reminiscing, he's hard to distract. I hope you found out what you came to learn."

"Yes, of course, and thank you, Mrs. Evans," Sally said quickly. "Perhaps you know something about Percy Landsman. Your husband was a bit vague."

"Nothing except what I read in the 'Style' section of *The Tribune.* Met him a few times, but . . ."

"Well, thank you anyway," Adam said.

She dismissed them with a vague wave of her hand, and they walked out to the car.

Sally drove out of the driveway and then pulled over onto the shoulder of the road a few hundred feet beyond the house. She gave Adam a strange look.

"What did you think?" he asked.

"If you want my honest opinion, I think he was exaggerating. Maybe so he wouldn't have to tell us anything. I didn't believe all that confusion for a minute. It seemed studied. I'll bet he's read up online somewhere about Alzheimer's symptoms and was just laying it on for our benefit. Maybe he knows a great deal about Landsman and just didn't want to say anything. And what did he mean calling him 'dark'?"

"I suppose you're right, Sally. I had the same impression, and I didn't like it. Did you notice his eyes? Completely alert . . . cunning even. So maybe he was putting it on. He may have mild memory loss, and who knows what the real diagnosis is, but nothing like that show he put on for us today. You don't descend into that kind of oblivion in a few weeks. Still, he managed to tell us a great deal. And I'll bet he knows more. So I'd say he's hiding something like Dwyer. Like they don't want anything to do with the will. And didn't he have a perfect excuse not to say another word, though? I'll have to remember that if the cops ever pull me over."

"Oh, Adam, you're so straight. I'll bet you never even got a parking ticket. Dream on. You wouldn't know how to be a crook."

"Don't underestimate me. I'm in a hurry, and sometimes you have to swerve around someone, especially if they're in your way."

"Well then, if you intend to drive, I'll buckle up."

Back in the office, Adam and Sally sat across from each other at the small table kitty-corner to his desk, piles of paper and notes in front of them.

"Do you want a coffee?" she asked.

"Yeah, but let me get it. You look over pages 3 and 4 again, where the beneficiaries are listed. We need to get going on finding that other person."

He stood up and left the room, and when he returned, he was carrying two mugs precariously gripped in one hand and a couple of bags of chips in the other.

"My treat," he said, spilling some of the coffee on the table as he set it down.

"Ever so generous . . . and careless! But listen, we've still got a problem. That woman at this address in the will and a phone number, but they don't seem accurate, or at least no one answers. I've tried calling—no answer. And I've sent out a registered letter but no response either."

"Then we'll have to drive down to that address and see if any neighbors know where she is. Unless you can think of a better way to locate her."

"OK. But perhaps not yet. Don't you think the brother comes first?"

"Sure, but before we do anything more, I want to read those letter attachments again. What in the world do you think they mean? I've been over them several times, and I still don't know why he included them, and apparently against the advice of Bill Evans. There's a note to that effect included in the file."

Adam picked up a single sheet. They are both to get copies.

"Read it out loud again. Maybe hearing it will help."

"OK," he said. "'To My Executor: This letter expresses my feelings and reasons for certain decisions made in my will.' I'm going to skip over this boilerplate in the first paragraph. It just affirms that it's an interpretation but doesn't change instructions about the property dispersal or anything else and stresses that the will is the only legal document. Anyway, here's the part that's so baffling and tentative: 'Each of you, my beneficiaries, is deserving of some explanation for the settlement I am bestowing upon you. I realize, in one case, that there is no way that a cash payment can undo the harm I have done and the mistakes I've made in my relationships. In the other, I am simply following my filial obligation, which I feel compelled to fulfill to my brother by adoption. But I hope that both parties will look generously on my original birth family if they can be located.'"

"The curse of confusion," Sally said.

"Exactly. Or an amendment to set things right. Whatever he intended, I can't imagine anything but confusion. What the hell did he think he gained? He just invited litigation by leaving such a loose end. No wonder Evans advised him not to include it. And do you suppose it was an invitation to find them? But you know, a will is supposed to be something final—a period at the end of a life's story. A last testament. But this? It just invites continuing trouble. And a challenge for someone to discover what he intended by that mention of his birth family."

He paused and frowned. "And I'll bet that's exactly what Dwyer was warning me not to do: locate the original birth family. I don't like that."

"And now you're thinking you just might be the one who's going to find them. And if you do? What then?"

"I have no idea. But I'm guessing you're just as curious as I am."

Chapter 4

Percy Landsman's brother lived on the twentieth story of a tall apartment building on East Riverside Drive, where it jutted out along the south bank of the Chicago River, with a view looking out over Lake Shore Drive and onto the flat plain of Lake Michigan. Adam imagined that if he looked through one of the enormous glass windows that faced east on a clear, calm summer's day, there would be yachts and sailboats plying across the horizon or scooting past the narrow opening into the harbor. In the other direction, from a window toward the north, there would be tour boats meandering slowly past the great architectural sights lining the river. And if one stepped onto the small, windy balcony and looked down, there would be the park and the silent stream of traffic on the highway crossing the Outer Drive Bridge and traveling north.

He and Sally had walked to the building from the law office, only a few blocks away, but he thought it was like emerging from a raucous factory town of pedestrians, cars, and buses—the grime of business and trade everywhere and covered over in the dark shadow by the Elevated— out into the calm of a magnificent castle park.

"A different world," he mumbled when Sally pointed to the building.

"You'd like to live here, though, wouldn't you?" she said as they approached the gleaming entrance. "Sell your soul for a plate glass view of the lake, maybe? Or better, just become a partner at Dwyer and Smithson."

"Pretty much the same thing," he said and watched her face for the smile that didn't appear.

Percy Landsman's brother had agreed to see them but insisted that he was too busy to come to the law office.

"There's something about being on your own terrain," Sally had remarked.

"Especially if you want the upper hand. Makes us the supplicants," Adam said.

"Except that you're the executor."

"But he'll certainly have the story to tell about his brother—if he's willing. So I guess that makes us even."

The entry to the condo building was surveyed by the doorman standing inside a small glassed-in compartment that opened into the lobby. Taking their names, he called up to the apartment and then pressed a buzzer that opened the doorway. Inside, the décor was muted shades of gray with a dark-blue carpet, an ensemble that whispered anonymous luxury. A bank of elevators was set off to the left, next to a corridor that led toward the back and, presumably, some sort of service area or possibly a gym or offices.

The apartment was located halfway down a curved hallway on the top floor of the building. Eric Landsman opened the door almost as soon as Adam dropped the heavy knocker. A shadow backlit against the bright sunlight streaming into the apartment behind him. He looked slightly unreal until he backed away to let them enter. A man of medium height, with close-cropped gray hair and ruddy skin, he held himself in an athletic posture. He was wearing maroon fleece pants and a matching sweatshirt as if he might be about to leave for a jog along the lakefront trail that ran along the front of the building.

"Come in and sit down," he said, turning and walking to a sofa that backed onto the gleaming east window.

They followed him, and when he pointed, they settled onto a matching sofa directly opposite and faced into the bright, almost blinding sunlight.

This was the theater of dominance, Adam said to himself. And he squinted at Sally to register his disgust.

"I'm not sure why you wanted to speak to me," Landsman began. "I thought that the will was straightforward—at least as far as I'm concerned. Was it you who called me, miss? To give me a preliminary on the bequest."

"Yes," Sally replied.

"Then I don't understand why you're here."

"We appreciate your taking the time to see us," Adam replied quickly. "There are just a few loose ends—partly because your brother's assets are complex and because, for example, the other beneficiary has been difficult to locate. You may be able to enlighten us."

"If I can."

Adam reached into the briefcase he had set on the floor, opened it, and extracted a single sheet. Standing up, he handed it to Landsman. "Perhaps you can tell us something about this person: Ida Wilmot. She's the other beneficiary besides yourself and some charities."

Landsman seized the paper and glanced at it, and then he shook his head. "I don't know her or what Percy might have had to do with her."

"Are you sure?" Sally asked.

"Absolutely," he said, standing to hand it back. "I can't help you. You see, Percy and I didn't have much to do with each other of late. For a long time, actually."

"But maybe you could tell us about him. It might give us a clue," Sally said.

"You want the full story, then? It'll take me a while."

"Yes, please."

Landsman smiled as if he had just scored a goal in some fanciful game. He leaned back and began: "I should say, first off, that Percy and I are only brothers by law. I don't know what you call it. Anyway, he was adopted, older than me by several years, and I guess that makes me the only natural son. Don't know what else to call us. I didn't understand about Percy when I was younger, although I sometimes wondered why our appearances and personalities were so different. But my parents never said much until . . . I think it was sophomore year in high school that I found out, although the date doesn't matter much.

"Anyway, I finally asked my mother one day because it was becoming really obvious to me that we were different and also because they treated us differently. Don't know why I chose that particular moment. But she wouldn't tell me—just said: 'Go ask your father.' But her tone was so sharp, angry almost, that I was almost afraid to. Except that I did, finally. And I got part of the story. But only enough to ask more questions. You know, in those days, people didn't want to talk about something so unnatural.

"So it turns out Percy was an adopted bastard. Our housekeeper—a Latino woman. I never knew her name. Long before my time. Anyway, I understand that she died in childbirth, some unknown father, and I guess my father felt sympathetic for some reason and took in the baby, insisted on it. Crazy thing to do. I don't think my mother ever forgave him, and you could see she resented . . . no, I think she came to hate Percy. At least she was always picking on him. It was like having two mothers in the same room, just depended on the direction she looked, what attitude she assumed, and how she spoke to us.

"I think you can imagine what that did to him, what became of him. It took me years to understand why I disliked him so much. I guess I was reflecting my mother's second-hand aversion. It was really awful, and it made him into a mean kid. He knew he was a splinter in the relationship of my parents—a dull and constant pain. And the worst thing was, he was older than me. My older half-brother. Aren't they supposed to look out for you? Well, maybe he did—in a way, yes. But I sure didn't want him hovering over me. I didn't want to be like him. Ever!

"But he was also determined. I've never met anyone as determined as he was—like all the obstacles in his life gave him energy, made him independent and secretive and ambitious. Of course, my dad tried but only half-heartedly. But I really didn't have a brother at all, just some stray kid, picked up from the shelter, so to speak. A bastard in every sense.

"I guess it was never good for him, but even worse when I came along. Since he was older than me, he was a lot stronger and angry all the time—angry at me and the world. So he took every opportunity to hurt me. It didn't bother him to be punished. He just accepted it as the price of—I don't know what—some kind of revenge. Wrecked my possessions whenever he got a chance, stole things: a real cuckoo in the nest. Always clamoring for attention, and it didn't matter if all he got was the back of the hand. For a while, I was sure he would have killed me if he had the chance."

"I don't understand," Sally broke in. "Why in the world, after all this, did he leave you a bequest? Unless you had some sort of reconciliation."

"No, we never got along, even at the end when he was sick. I rarely saw him. Didn't want to. But my guess is that he wanted to avoid a lawsuit. Clever of him. You know, I'm legally a brother, and if he left me out of the will, I could sue. I'm sure you know that it's complicated to disinherit a close relative. So he put me in just out of spite. Tossed me a bone with just enough meat on it to keep me chewing. And anyway, even if it's a lot, according to what you wrote to me, I don't really need it. But maybe, if he hadn't, I would have liked to get back at him—drag his lousy corpse into court."

Adam looked at Sally, trying to signal his surprise, but she just looked away.

"Just out of curiosity, I'm wondering if you know anything about his mother—who she was? There's a note appended to the will mentioning his birth mother, her family. I'm sure the lawyer shared it with you."

"Do you think I give a damn about them? Anyway, she was long dead when I came along." Landsman said, half getting up from his seat and then settling back again. "A bastard is a bastard. Family or no family."

"But if there was another family, perhaps they might have some claims on the will, or if not, wouldn't it be a good idea to inform them about his death?" Sally asked.

"Why would I want to do that? They have no business with us, whoever they are, and certainly no claim to anything. I don't care what Percy wanted."

"In a purely legal sense, you're probably right, Mr. Landsman," Adam said.

"In that case, I believe our business is done," Landsman said. "I'll expect to hear from you when the will is officially probated." He stood up and, without waiting for any response, walked toward the door to show them out.

"Thanks very much for your time, Mr. Landsman," Adam said. "Of course, I'll be in touch."

He and Sally walked out, and the door closed behind them with just enough force to make the point that, for Landsman, the interview had been unpleasant and was now happily over.

As they walked toward the elevator, Adam said, "Why did you say something about a claim on the will? You know that isn't likely. His mother, the maid, died in childbirth. And the family, probably impossible to find. And nothing in that letter is legally binding."

"I know," she said, touching his arm gently so he would look at her. "But what a delicious reaction I got! Such an unpleasant man. I couldn't resist ruffling his fur."

"Be careful about rubbing a cat the wrong way. You'll get clawed," Adam said. "And I really don't want him to complain to the firm about us, except, of course, that you're right. It was worth knowing how intensely he felt about his brother, even if it's just a useless bit of information to store away."

"You never know," she said, stopping at the elevator to push the down button. "I keep a mental note of lots of useless information, and you'd be surprised."

"Should I be worried, then? I mean about myself?" he said.

"Absolutely! You've got a bulging file."

Back in the lower reaches of the firm, Adam and Sally sat in his office. It was after hours, and the partners had all left from home, but several of the juniors remained, well into their sixty-hour workweek. Although all the lights were on, it seemed to Adam as if the gathering dusk outside had leached into the room, creating shadows where there should be none. He said nothing except to chide himself for his gloomy mood.

"You know," said Sally, sitting straight in her chair at the conference table, "I'm beginning to wonder what a normal person does with all that leisure time they have. It must be boring to have a life. I mean, I'd be almost at loose ends to fill up the days and weekends. What to cook that didn't come in a box? See friends, just hang out in a museum? What's that all about?"

"You knew what you were signing on for, Sally. It's just a matter of serving your time."

"Easy for you to say, Adam. You're on the fast track. Their fair-haired boy. But I don't see much advancement from my position."

"Look, Sally," he said, "you're really good at what you do. I'm sure that they'll put you in a regular slot sometime. Just stick with it."

"Maybe I'm too good where I am, and they won't want to move me."

"Then you've got a serious complaint. They'd have to realize that."

"I don't know, Adam. I mean, how many women have made partner?"

"None so far, I'll grant you, but—"

"But nothing! Those good old boys aren't about to open that door for me. Think of the changes they'd have to make, and I don't just mean refurbishing the bathrooms on the second floor. Maybe have to install an all-gender john! Can you imagine that one? Or invite me to play golf? I wonder which they'd think was worse."

"I admit you'd be a terrible disruption," he said. "I can just imagine. Someone competent, outgoing, ambitious, and female." He didn't add that she was a remarkably handsome woman. Yes, they would fall all over themselves to open doors for her—but probably not *that* door.

"And without a Winnetka pedigree!" she added.

"But I come from nowhere too," he said. "And that makes me wonder why they made me co-executor of the will. It's almost as if they planned something. Why else engineer it so someone inexperienced is in charge of a complicated legal document?"

"Maybe they thought you'd just go by the book or ask for guidance when things became difficult with Bill Evans incapacitated."

"In other words, keep whatever they're hiding out of view, counting on my incompetence to seal up a secret—if there is one."

"You're awfully suspicious, Adam. But maybe you're right."

"Or maybe I'm just inventing a story because I like mysteries."

"I'd say there's something to your suspicions. Look at how evasive Bill Evans was. We spent a half hour with him, and he didn't tell us anything we didn't already know. And pretending to forget every time we asked him a question."

"Unless there's nothing to tell."

"And that will is straightforward? If so, why have we had such difficulty locating the money and finding that other beneficiary? But there's that nagging addendum about his family—if they even exist."

"I think there has to be an innocent explanation for all this. Except that we need to find the other beneficiary first."

"Just a name and address that seems to be outdated."

"I know you tried. So maybe it's time to visit that address, see if we can run her down."

"You make that sound like you're on a mission of vengeance," she laughed.

"Maybe I am. So let me see where it is."

Sally opened the copy of the will that lay on the table in front of them and turned to the page listing the beneficiaries.

"Last whereabouts was on the near South Side."

"Why don't we pay her a visit or talk to the neighbors to find out where she's gone?" he said.

"Now?"

"Yep. Grab your coat."

Half an hour later, Adam was maneuvering Sally's car through the late afternoon end-to-end traffic streaming along Lake Shore Drive.

"Remind me never to drive anywhere after two at the latest."

"Don't ever drive anywhere after two!" she said quickly.

"Great advice, Sally, and timely too. Wish I had listened to you."

"You can always count on me for judicious instruction."

He looked over at her and smiled because he really didn't mind the stop and go so long as she was sitting next to him. And he also liked looking out across the oncoming lane of cars toward the lake—steel gray and ruffled in the slanted afternoon sun. This miraculous body of water was, he thought, the savior of the city rising up from the dull, flat plain of the Midwest, looking to the edge of a limitless horizon—a horizon of endless possibilities—like a coastal port, open to all the exotic places of the imagination—even if it was bounded on the other side by monotonous miles of corn fields, hog farms, and muddy rivers. Chicago was a city that somehow shouldn't be there, except that it was.

"Get off somewhere around here," she said suddenly. "The address is on Dearborn, around 35th Street."

He turned at the next exit and drove west a few blocks into the neighborhood.

"Ever been out here before?" he asked after they slowed.

"No. No reason to, but this building looks familiar."

"It's probably the apartment or condo—generic anonymous, all over the city," he said, pulling up in front of a brown three-story brick construction.

He parked, and they got out and walked up the steps to the front door. To the right was a callbox, and Adam found the name Wilmot and pressed the button next to it. They waited.

"I can't believe the name is still here," he said. "If she still lives here, I wonder why she never answered your letters or calls."

"I have no idea. Something's not right, for sure."

"She's probably not home—long gone," Sally said after a moment. "Did you ever notice that every time a detective on a TV show or in a movie calls on a suspect, they are invariably at home?"

"Or if not, the door will be ajar, right? And they barge in and find a body with a knife sticking in his chest."

He pressed the button again, harder this time as if he could make it sound louder.

Again, there was no response.

"OK, let's try one of the other neighbors," Adam said. He touched the button just below hers, and almost immediately, a voice answered.

Adam didn't wait but said, "This is Adam Chauncey. I'm a lawyer, and I'm trying to find Ms. Ida Wilmot. Could I speak to you?"

"You got business with her? OK. I'll let you in. She's probably there. She don't never answer. But I'll let you in."

The door buzzed, and Adam pushed it open, and they entered a small, cramped hallway with a door on either side and a staircase in the middle. No elevator.

"Two A, so up one flight, I think," Adam said, leading the way.

The second-floor landing was also small and dingy, with a worn gray carpet. Several shoes lay in front of one of the apartment doors. The only illumination was the afternoon light filtered through a dirty window.

Adam knocked on the opposite side and waited. He could hear a muffled sound, and he assumed that someone inside was peering out of the peephole and deciding whether or not to let them in.

Adam smiled as if that would assure her.

The door opened about two inches, restrained by a heavy brass chain. He could barely see the person, but he was sure that he and Sally were being carefully assessed.

"Ms. Wilmot. We've come about the will of the late Percy Landsman. My name is Adam Chauncey, and this is my assistant, Sally Warren. We represent the law firm of Smithson and Dwyer." He smiled again.

The door closed and then swung wide.

"Thought it might be some joke," said the woman standing in the doorframe. "You wouldn't be surprised at what they'll do to get into your apartment these days, even when I've got nothing worth taking. But sometimes that's not even the point anymore, is it?"

"Can we come in?" Adam said, stepping forward.

"If it'll make you happy. I suppose so."

The two of them followed her into the apartment, through a hallway and into a living room.

"Sit down over there," she said, pointing to the small, low sofa covered in faded chintz that sat at right angles to an unused fireplace. She took an upright armchair facing them, and Adam had the momentary feeling that this was going to be an interrogation.

"I'm wondering if you got my telephone call or the registered letter I sent to you," Sally asked.

"Yep, got 'em both."

"Is there some reason you didn't answer?"

"Sure there is. I didn't want to have anything more to do with Percy Landsman or any other Landsman you might be representing. And if it means that he's dead, why then, good riddance, I say."

Adam had said nothing, but instead, he found himself staring intently at her. She was elderly, but he couldn't guess her age (he never was good at that). Perhaps seventy or maybe more. She had severely dyed brown hair that looked unnaturally uniform, luminous, and dark against the taut, shiny skin of her forehead. She was wearing an expensive-looking sweater with sequins sewn in scallops along the sides and a full dark skirt. He wondered if this was the sort of person who dressed every day in expectation of some outing . . . but never went out, never answered the phone, never saw anyone, and never left the apartment. That would be remarkably strange—almost as odd as the strange and incongruous impression she made. Why did he think that?

"Could you tell us how you knew Mr. Landsman?" Sally said.

"Knew him? A long time ago. I suppose as well as anyone could or would ever want to. Yes, I could tell you a thing or two."

Sally settled into her chair, visibly relaxing, Adam thought, as if preparing to hear a long story. It was a clever gesture, and he wondered if the woman sitting across from her would respond.

"I met Percy a long time ago, seems like I've always known him. I don't remember exactly when it was, and we always disagreed about that. He insisted that he picked me up at a bar. Not likely! Laughed about it, but it made me feel cheap."

She sat straighter, and her voice sounded firmer: "No, I don't remember it that way at all. He had a way of making you feel dependent, under his control. To this day, I can't tell you why he was so attractive. Handsome, very dark, sure, but lots of men like that can be attractive. But he was sinister, too, in a way that could make you shudder. At least when I knew him. What's the word for that? Enthralling? Fascinating? I don't think that fits because you also felt a kind of danger surrounding him. I'm not good at descriptions, and I'm searching here. Driven."

"Sadistic?" Sally said quietly.

"Like that, but no, not really. I think that word means something permanent, like a character flaw, and I always thought Percy might just be acting. Maybe that's why I stayed with him so long."

"So you had a relationship?"

"Yes, young man, that's what I'm telling you. You don't have to coax me. I'll tell you in my own way." She sounded angry now. "So just stop interrupting."

"Of course," he said.

"Anyway, it was a long time ago. Percy and I lived together for almost ten years when we were both fairly young—not that I counted up anniversaries or anything like that or kept old datebooks. He sure would have laughed at such sentimentalism. And during that whole time, I don't think I ever really knew him. He didn't talk about his business much, although I know it had to do with investments. Flashed a lot of money around toward the end. And that family? If you touched on the subject of his parents, you'd get burned. But you'd think he was raised an orphan or put out in some group home, like in a shelter or something, the way he talked. Then every once in a while, he'd disappear or not tell me where he had been, and I always thought he was with them—whoever they were—partly because afterward, he'd seem so angry or hurt or some crazy combination of feelings that just didn't go together."

She paused. "I can tell you that he was adopted. Told me that once and then said never to mention it again—like it was some kind of secret or a flaw, like a birthmark. Treated it like a defect or something. Maybe he thought it was a key to who he was, something deep and bitter, and he didn't want you to see it. Also told me once he had a brother. But I don't know anything more about them. I mean the father and mother. Anyway, we were together for a long time, but I knew from the start that we'd never get married. He wasn't like that. I thought he hated the idea of families. Surprised me a while back when I found out he got married. Wouldn't have thought it."

She paused and leaned forward in her chair as if to confide some secret: "And you know, he hated that name of his. Said it wasn't him. That his parents tried to make him into a person called Percy when he wanted to be someone else. I guess I felt sorry for him sometimes. Complicated man. And then, one day, he just disappeared. Walked away, left his clothes in the apartment we shared, and I never saw him again. Heard some things, but he was gone. I'm surprised he wanted to remember. And me, well, I just wanted to forget."

She stopped and smoothed her skirt and then crossed her legs and began again: "At first, I was furious and maybe a bit desperate, but then I found out he had put this apartment in my name. Got a letter from some lawyer—could have been your firm, I don't remember—describing the transaction. Probably was that he felt guilty. Who knows? But that was it. Never saw the bastard again."

She looked at Adam for a moment. "And now you tell me he's left a bequest. Sure, I read that letter you guys sent me. After all these years? That's got to be guilt money, and I don't want it. That's why I didn't answer you. What am I supposed to do? Forgive his memory? No, sir. Took the installment plan to get rid of him. You know, I allowed myself a little bit of anger and grief once in a while until it was finally all paid out. Do you think I want it all coming back now? The memories. Except that, I guess, in his mind it wasn't really over. What a rat to bring up all those things I haven't thought of for years."

She started to stand and then sat back again. "So, you can keep your money, and you can leave now."

"You could still accept the bequest, Ms. Wilmot. Give it to some charity. We're obligated to disperse it, whether you want it or not, you know," Sally said.

"And then I'll have to pay taxes on it? Right? Just like him to pull a stunt like that! OK, I could give it away, I suppose. So why don't you send me a check? And maybe it'll get lost in the mail or torn up and too damaged to cash. Too bad I can't just write 'Return to sender,' except that the paper it's written on would burn up when it got to where he's gone. Now leave, you two, and don't bother to come back."

"There's one more thing before we go," Adam said, walking toward the door. "Did he ever mention wanting to find his birth family? Who his real father was?"

"Seems like he did once or twice. Yes."

"And did he ever find them?" Sally asked.

"No. I'm sure he didn't. At least he never said." She stood up and put her hands on her hips.

"Now, please leave."

Back in the car, dodging in and out of traffic, Sally had insisted on driving. They headed back up toward the Loop. Above and around them, the dying sun on the horizon had transformed a thin layer of cloud to a dim red with only a tip of pale blue etched on the eastern edge. The way it always did, the lake anticipated nightfall, turning an opaque dark against the inadequate light. Traffic pouring out of the city jammed the opposite lane.

"Promise me you won't die, Adam," Sally exclaimed as she swerved to the right around a particularly slow vehicle occupying the fast lane.

"If you slow down, I think I'll probably live a while longer."

"Not what I meant. It's the bother and complication of it. Tracking down the beneficiaries, uncovering the funds, filing documents with the court, waiting for probate, and of course, in this case disposing of Landsman's complicated legacy."

"You're right," he said. "It seems like it takes months to die completely nowadays. Sell the property, liquidate or give away the contents of a large house. And in his case, a large apartment. Find his heirs. Maybe also, in this case, deal with all his guilt."

"It does sound like he was trying to make amends."

"Yes, with a cash amendment."

"That might make me angry, too, if that's all a memory was worth," she said, glancing briefly at him. "To change the subject, I assume we'll get an accounting from that concierge management outfit I hired to dispose of his possessions. Expecting it very soon."

"You're talking about Cull and Plunder, Incorporated, I assume?"

"Very funny, Adam. But whatever you call them, you'll still have to go through all his papers. They obviously won't touch them."

Sally suddenly leaned back and stiff-armed the horn as a large, black SUV cut them off.

"I have just one word for your driving," Adam said as he reached up and clutched the grab handle above the door: "Slow down."

"That's two words. And don't worry, I'll get us back to the office safe and sound."

"Well, if we survive," he said, "maybe you'd like to have dinner tonight. There's a couple of new places I'd like to try out. Near you."

"So you've been scouting out the area. But I don't think so. Not tonight, Adam. Sorry, I have other plans."

He turned and looked at her tense profile. It reminded him about the strangeness of talking to someone in a car, where both of them, sitting just a foot apart, almost touching, would be looking forward out the windshield as if conversing with some unseen third person hovering on the front hood. He was tempted to reach over and touch her shoulder just to break this odd triangulation. But he said nothing more and stared again at the gleaming taillights of the cars in front of them.

Chapter 5

Adam stumbled into his office late the next morning and sat down hard in his chair behind the desk. When he finally made it home the previous night, he had lounged in the living room of his apartment, stretched out on the sofa, thumbing the remote of his TV past programs he had no interest in watching. There was nothing but amateur competitions, sports rebroadcasts, endless advertising, and on PBS a beg-a-thon with some guru promising longer life if you just followed his diet (and bought his expensive book). On the table in front of him was a novel he had tried to read, but that wasn't doze-proof either, so he drank too many shots of scotch. He had been too bored and restless to go to bed, and now, this morning, he regretted the waste of his evening and his struggle to sleep on the couch that bent him to its shape.

"Nice morning," Sally said absently as she walked into the room without knocking. And then she stopped. "But you look like you wouldn't have noticed the balmy weather. What happened to you last night?"

"Well," he said, looking up at her. "There was this girl I had a fancy to take to dinner, but she turned me down, cold. So I drowned my sorrows in whiskey."

"Poor Adam, and shame on that person, whoever she was!"

"My thought exactly."

"Do you think you're up to talking about the Landsman will? Or should I get you some coffee first?"

"No, I'm fine. And I'll get us the coffee. Won't be a minute. You sit."

He got up slowly and walked into the small lounge, put a small sealed packet of grounds in the machine, pressed a button, and waited as a thin stream of brown liquid sputtered into the plastic cup he held. He set that aside and then repeated it a second time.

"Coffee served," he said, returning to the office and placing the cup in front of her on the conference table.

"You know, Adam, you don't have to prove you're not a male chauvinist."

"I know, but sometimes I think I could use the practice," he said, joining her.

She took a sip of her drink and then opened the file she had placed in front of her. Adam thought, all business this morning, but he couldn't help noticing the faint scent of perfume. And he had to ask himself if the blouse she was wearing was tighter than usual or whether it was just the alcohol still rampaging in his system and playing tricks on his vision.

"You don't have to take my advice, Adam, but I think we ought to go through some of the papers that are still in the apartment. That is if you're up to it." She studied his face for a moment and then continued.

"Because, as of this morning, I haven't received anything more about the assets. And I'm still waiting to hear from one of the charities he mentions. What do you say?"

"Glad you're on top of the details, Sally. And I agree. Let's go over to the apartment and sift through his papers. I'm not optimistic, or rather, I'm kind of doubtful that we'll discover much. But just in case we find there's something else we need to do."

"Good. I'll grab my jacket."

"And I'll let you drive again if you don't mind. You have the address?"

"Yes. North Side. Up just north of Boys Town."

"You don't suppose . . . ?"

"I don't suppose anything," she said. "Just as likely he was a baseball fan. Only a few blocks to Wrigley Field, isn't it? Let's go. And maybe you ought to leave your assumptions behind in the office."

Landsman's house was set in a block of semi-attached townhouses on West Addison. There was a slim yard on one side that only emphasized the narrowness of the structure. Like many older Chicago dwellings, it was constructed of gray limestone, rusticated to give it a fortress-like appearance, but with broad windows, and at the landing up a cast-iron staircase, an arched entrance with heavy-set pillars and a dark oak door.

"I wonder what the architect was thinking when he designed such a monstrosity," Sally said as they climbed, her heels clanging on the steps. "Except I wonder if there even was an architect. It seems to me I've seen this same house all over Chicago."

"And I wonder why anyone would buy it. Sort of a house that's thumbing its nose at the idea of a city, don't you think?"

"Well, it certainly isn't welcoming, even if it has a kind of medieval charm. Makes me wonder about our owner."

"I guess we'll find out shortly," Adam said, pulling a small wallet of keys out of his pocket and selecting the largest one to insert into the lock.

The interior hall, once they stepped inside, was an odd contest of brilliant colors from a stained-glass skylight and gloomy shadows that played on the ceramic floor.

"It looks as if every piece of furniture has some sort of tag on it," Sally commented as they walked into the living room. Reading what was written on several, she said, "Everything seems to be destined either for sale or to give away. Those concierge people are thorough, that's for sure. I'm glad they're doing the sorting and not me."

"Feels slightly creepy to me," Adam said, "having your life divided between what's worth keeping and what's going to be junked."

"I guess that's the way it is in the end," she said. "We're all pack rats of the inconsequential."

"And I suppose you can tell a lot about a person by the objects he surrounded himself with."

"Maybe. But I will say one thing, though," she said after they looked around briefly in the kitchen and then walked through the sparsely furnished dining room. "So far, this house doesn't seem to have an individual touch. If I had to, I'd say that the décor is early modern anonymous with all the charm of a dentist's reception! Reminds me of something I heard once: 'You are what you own.' But what does a dark leather couch tell you or a kitchen where all the storage shelves are bare? Does it mean the person had a morose personality? Or maybe just liked to eat out? I hesitate to imagine what people would think about me if they went through my possessions!"

Adam wanted to reply that any careful observer would conclude that she was a free spirit, an amusing companion, smart and ambitious, and very private. But he kept these thoughts to himself.

But he was curious about what she said and grabbed her arm. "Do you really think that possessions make the man . . . or woman? Such an odd thing to say. Who are you anyway? I'm confused about all your contradictions."

"Sorry, Adam. It's just that it strikes me that so far, we've seen nothing but necessities and simplicity. No effort to make this place a home. Maybe I chose the wrong words, but you have to agree that it's odd that there are few personal touches anywhere in sight. Of course, it's possible we'll find an office upstairs filled with family photographs that line the walls, his first finger paintings from kindergarten, school yearbooks, and his favorite teddy bear, but somehow I doubt that. I think it's going to remain a puzzle to figure out who he was."

It seemed for a moment to Sally that she could be talking about herself. Not, of course, that she had surrounded herself with mementos of a happy childhood. Because that hadn't been entirely the case. What she remembered most was having two bedrooms: one at her father's apartment and one in the home that her mother retained after the divorce. Both had remarried, and she had been shuttled—shunted, in fact—between identities, a doubled-up daughter in two blended families (that's the going term for it now, she understood), except that she had always felt like the mismatched intruder in both places. So she wouldn't have known which set of stuffed animals and posters really made up her past, and she had abandoned all of them the way she had sloughed off her adolescence. And that instability undoubtedly made her skittish about relationships. Not that she hadn't had opportunities. But nothing ever worked out quite right, and now here was Adam, the innocent, gangly young lawyer from Carbondale who seemed to be as conflicted about himself as she was in him wanting to ask her out. She was pretty sure she could see a blinking yellow signal that warned her of an approaching red light.

"Well, luckily, we really don't have to figure him out, much as I'd like to," Adam said. "Our job—my job—is just to see that the property is liquidated and the terms of the will are fulfilled, nothing more, except . . ."

"So is there some mystery here or not, do you think?"

"I really don't know, Sally. I really don't," he said, leading the way out into the hallway again.

At the top of a steep staircase, they entered into what looked like the master bedroom and then a small adjacent den with a sofa and a television set. The final room on the opposite side of the landing was a complete surprise. Rather than sparse, Landsman's office was filled with piles of books, cabinets, and on the desk, several loose papers, neatly stacked files and notepads, with a cleared space at the center.

"It looks like he was working on something . . . or about to," Sally said, looking around the room. "Still nothing really personal, except maybe what's in the papers. You'd expect a memento or two, I suppose."

"No doubt," Adam said, sitting down at the desk and reaching over to turn on the lamp.

"I'm going to empty the drawers of the desk and look through these files. I'll hand anything I think is interesting to you. Probably nothing consequential, but who knows?"

"Sure," she said. "I'll make a space on the floor."

"Are you sure?" he asked. "Maybe you could find a portable table or something."

"Good idea. I'll look," she said, walking over to a closet, which she opened. "Nothing here. I'll be back. Maybe I'll find something in one of the other rooms."

She left, and Adam could hear doors opening and shutting. Odd, he thought, how the house echoed as if it were half empty.

He turned back and began to look through the files. He was surprised to find them neatly labeled and the papers inside them either stapled or clipped together. Most, as he opened them, were bills of one sort or another and some business correspondence. But anything truly personal, he thought, would probably be on a computer or cell phone, although neither was in sight. Besides, he didn't have any passwords. If he couldn't find those and if Landsman had neglected to write them down, it would be nearly impossible to access his private communications—if that proved necessary.

But going through all the papers that he took from the desk, he finally discovered, at the very bottom of a neat pile in the bottom drawer, a folder labeled *passwords*. Glancing through it, he found that about half of the entries were abbreviations: they could be banks or insurance companies, almost anything. The rest seemed to be a miscellany of credit cards, airline accounts, and online apps. Nothing terribly interesting, although he'd have to go through everything to see if there were any hidden accounts.

On the left, he found a single folder marked "Will." Adam opened it and was surprised to find several pages of handwritten notes and several post-its and, beneath this, a facsimile of the familiar document that had been consigned to Smithson and Dwyer. Turning to the last page, he found his signature.

Landsman had a very careful hand, with some odd swirls on capital letters. But it was plain, at a glance, that the other papers and notes in this folder were notes for the will. But just to make sure, he'd need to compare the finished document with these pages to see if they matched.

No doubt, he speculated, these were probably just old scribblings that Landsman had used in preparing his bequests. But almost immediately, as he began to read more carefully, he found something entirely different and absolutely contrary to the final testament that had been prepared by his firm. These scrawled bits contained several versions of beneficiaries, with only a single letter designating a person next to percentages that shifted around with each entry. Unfortunately, there were no dates on any of these notes, so it was unclear if they preceded or came after the original will—and probably no way to find out which came first, if that became an issue.

He suddenly became aware that Sally had reentered the room.

"This is really curious," he said, not looking over to where she was standing.

"What's curious is the way you begin a sentence and stop halfway through," she replied, replacing what she was looking at and turning in his direction. "How about letting me in on the other half?"

"This odd file . . . marked 'will,' which contains a copy of the document I signed, but then there is a series of notes as if he was playing around with bequests and hadn't decided on who got what. Like he couldn't make up his mind. And, apparently, different amounts."

"But he did decide, eventually, right? So what's the problem?"

"Perhaps nothing. Except that some of the notes refer to individuals that weren't named in the final will."

"That doesn't make any sense," she said, standing up and walking over to peer over his shoulder. "But does it really matter?"

"Probably not. But judging from the arrangement of the papers, there's something odd. If you think in geological terms, the finished, final will ought to come first—top stratum—but the notes seem to be more recently piled on top. Wouldn't you put the finished will in last if that was your final thought?"

"I don't know what he would do. This guy's an enigma to me, but aren't you inventing a problem? I can think of lots of reasons why the papers are in that order. On the other hand, is there any indication of who he was thinking about making a beneficiary?"

"Yes. There's an *E* I think for Eric, his brother, and then an *I* for Ida Wilmot. But there's also a couple of *S*'s, some unknown persons. Damn, this guy had a thing for abbreviations!"

Adam pushed the file to the side of the desk where she could see it better. For a moment, he hoped she would put a hand on his shoulder and then lean over closer, but instead, she backed away and then pulled a chair up to the desk.

"Let me see," she said, picking up the pile of notes and looking through them carefully.

"I'm sure you're right," she said, holding up a half-page that she had just unfolded. "You missed this. See, the names are spelled out here: there is a small bequest for his brother. And something for the old girlfriend we visited. But look at this. At the bottom, several people named Sanchez. That's the mysterious *S*. And the bulk of the estate goes to them."

Adam took the paper from her hand and looked at it. "Well, yes, you're right. And the bequests are very different. He's left almost nothing to his brother and everything to *S*. What the hell?"

"Maybe he was just planning to be mean and then thought better of it? Then made the will you signed."

"But who are these people? All of them have the same last name: Sanchez, Sanchez. But no addresses, no first names, and just some percentages. And all much larger than his own brother. I wonder if this is the family he referred to in that letter."

"So now," she said, turning to look at him, "you're going to ask me what we should do. And I haven't got the slightest idea. I'm not the lawyer here. But maybe I've got a few ideas. Just let me think. A couple of possibilities. It could be that he was contemplating a new will, and he's playing around with the changes. And then he decided against it. Or maybe it's something else that we won't ever discover. In any case, you'll have to choose—either ignore these worksheets and proceed as you were with the probate. Ignore that note about the family. Or we ask a lot of questions, possibly even find out that there's another will somewhere that might or might not be legal."

She stood up straight and backed away from the desk. It occurred to her that Adam was treating her as a kind of partner, asking for her advice, which she was giving freely—too freely, perhaps—for her position as a paralegal. After all, her job was just research. But wasn't it just like her, she thought, to step beyond the circumference of her job? Still he had invited her opinion, and what would be the result if she remained mum? He'd probably insist in any case.

"I have no idea what to do," he continued. "Seems there are two choices. We could just discount what we found today and make the firm its commission and bury our questions or try to find another document or even trace some of these people and find out why he was thinking of dividing his fortune among them."

"Depends on what you think you owe to the dead," she said. "And I'm not sure this character deserves that, and besides, he's not going to know."

"I'm not sure either. And I doubt very much he's watching over us from some heavenly sky box. But I'm curious. Who was Landsman, and more to the point, what's his relation to these people?"

"Then I suppose we ought to lug these documents back to the office. Are you going to mention this to any of the partners?"

"I don't think so, no," he replied. "We don't know what they mean yet, and I have this feeling that they'd prefer not to know upstairs."

"Aren't you being overly suspicious?"

"It's my nature, I guess. Reaction to an ill-starred childhood."

"Or maybe you just don't like the way the firm is run—all that hierarchy and privilege."

"Yeah, and their secret handshakes too!"

Sally said nothing as she stood up and walked down the stairs to the living room. She returned with a folded packing box.

"Put your doubts in here," she said, finally.

Adam looked at her, searching her face for a smile, but he thought he could only see a hint of irony.

"Fine," he said, opening the sides of the box. "We can come back again and look through the rest of his papers later. It's getting late, and I don't like to be away from the office for too long."

"Do you think we'll find anything more?"

"Probably not," he said, standing up, "unless it's just more confusion."

It was late afternoon when they emerged from the townhouse and walked in the fading light along the sidewalk toward the car. A cool, moist breeze off the lake had picked up the acrid odor of smog as it made its way across the city. Adam thought, *The smell of a Chicago spring, full of contradiction and broken promises.* He looked at Sally and decided to say nothing about his observation. Too poetic! He wasn't sure, but maybe he should let down his defenses with her, be willing to be *vulnerable*— that dreadful word that was making the rounds of TV talk shows and relationship advice columns. *Yeah, vulnerable,* he thought, *just one more arrow in the quiver of some guy desperate to score a hook-up.* Was that him? Would that solve the problem of his loneliness? Damn, he thought, being a junior lawyer had made him a hermit. He needed to get out of his cave.

He glanced at Sally walking by his side and then stopped abruptly.

"Why don't we stop for a drink somewhere? No need to rush back to the office. We can talk a bit about what to do next. And anyway, I'm thinking that I'd like to keep these documents at my apartment for the time being."

"OK, but I thought you needed to get back," she said.

"Changed my mind," he said, pausing to look at her.

"All right. Let's put this box in the trunk and walk on a bit. There's sure to be a café nearby. I think I saw a couple of places as we were driving in."

"Great," he said, and they continued the brief distance to the car.

Adam popped the trunk and placed the box inside, and then slammed it shut.

"Now," he said, "Let's figure out what to do with this puzzle."

"Or not," she replied.

They ambled on, past another block of row houses to the intersection with North Halsted. There were several establishments open, but they chose one with a large plate-glass window revealing an interior that, against the gathering dusk outside, gleamed with soft light. When they entered, Adam immediately sensed the lingering bittersweet smell of coffee. Above the low and muffled conversations of patrons scattered around the room at several tables, the whine of the coffee grinder rose and fell. After they placed their order, they found seats in a booth in the corner.

"So, what do you think?" Sally said, pulling her arms out of her coat and leaving her shoulders covered.

"To tell you the truth, I'm becoming convinced that he was contemplating a different will. Whether it was prior to the one I signed or something new, however, is the only question worth asking."

"That makes good sense. But how will we ever find out which, and more to the point, why should you bother?"

"Maybe just to show them—the partners, I mean. Maybe I'm wrong, but I have the feeling this was some kind of setup. You know, tag the junior associate with no experience, keen to please, just follow the book, sir! Get things done quickly. No questions asked."

"You think there's something shady going on?"

"I always think that."

"I think I hear a troubled childhood speaking again," she said, shrugging her coat off her shoulders.

Adam couldn't help staring at her, thinking how prim and proper she looked but sexy in her work clothes and unapproachable.

"Maybe you're right," he said, shaking his head. "So I'll tell you if you want. About my difficult family, that is. But only if I can find out more about you. You're the mysterious one here."

"There's not much to tell," she said.

"Then I'll hang on every word. Make each sentence count for two!"

She laughed and said, "OK. So you were describing your deprived childhood?"

"Mine was not really deprived so much as strange," he began. "My father died when I was very young. Never really knew much about him. The only memory I have of him is more like an elusive shadow, someone who was scarcely around and, when he was, silent and slightly scary. But I was only about five or so. And when he died, he apparently left us only the house—my mother and me and my younger brother. She took a job teaching school, although when I think back on it now, she's the last person I'd ever turn loose on children."

"Sounds grim."

"She wasn't cruel. I don't mean that. Not at all. But completely self-centered and high-strung. She must have been very beautiful once, surrounded by beaux, used to leading a precious life. That was her favorite word, by the way: *precious.* Told me once that my father used to carry her up the stairs to bed every night." He stopped. "Why would you ever tell a child something like that? No wonder I'm screwed up!"

"On the other hand . . ." He paused again. "You know it's impossible to judge the way your parents look to others, but I'd say she did and still does possess a kind of fragile loveliness. Jet-black hair even now, pink skin, the smell of violets, and always wearing variations of the same color: dark-red suits and dresses and all shades of lavender. Everything in her world— even the most awful setbacks and our poverty when I was growing up were only things for her to deny. In her eyes, the world was all a pleasant harmony and full of romance even when it so obviously wasn't. And I couldn't stand it. It was like trying to walk through a field of sweet-smelling glue. Sometimes I wanted to shout at her just for once to make her confront reality. But I never did. I just left. I guess that was the cowardly thing to do, but maybe for the best, in the long run, not to shatter her illusions."

"So you think that left you with none yourself," Sally interrupted.

"None?"

"Illusions."

"Yes, I suppose you're right. And maybe that explains why I went into law—grubby, boring, rigid law. The reality of a price paid."

"Except that now you think that it isn't so straightforward after all and that discovering a few scribblings has made you doubt everything: your firm, the motives of the partners, the honesty of everything. Aren't you exaggerating?"

"Damn you, Sally," he said, leaning back against the leatherette back of the booth. "A win for the prosecution. You're too good."

"Not at all," she said. "You're just an easy read."

"Yeah, like a book of cartoons and anything profound I might have to say could easily fit inside one of those speech bubbles."

"No, I'd say more like an open book."

"You'd be surprised what's between the covers," he said.

She suddenly stiffened. "Whoa! Careful now! I think that's enough for now. You're about to stray off the subject, and I don't like the direction you're heading."

"Sorry. But now that I've finished confessing, what about you?"

"Another time, I think," she said. "It is getting late. I will tell you one thing, however. Unlike you, I had too much family. Two mothers and fathers—steps and real. But maybe I've landed in the same spot as you."

"You mean a cautious life," he said.

"If you want to put it that way. And now I need to get back to the firm to sign out. I don't have the luxury you do."

"If by luxury you mean that juniors have no hours, in other words, no personal hours, OK. But I'll take a rain check on the rest of your story. Only fair."

"We'll see," she said, standing up and slipping her arms through the sleeves of her coat.

Adam hesitated for a moment and then joined her. He didn't want to think about how the day had left him with frayed expectations and a nagging sense of frustration.

That evening, back in his apartment, he sat in the living room on the sofa, a half-full glass of wine next to the box of documents he had placed on the table in front of him. Through the alcove, looking into the kitchen, he could see the white cartons of Chinese carry-out sitting open on the counter. He hadn't even bothered to dish out his dinner onto a plate. It was late, and he knew there would be nothing worthwhile on television. He leaned over to grab the cell phone that lay next to him and started to dial Sally, and then he tossed it back down. He knew it would be wrong to call her at this hour. But he couldn't help himself. He picked it up again and punched in the numbers.

She answered, and he started to talk immediately without a word of apology.

"Something's been bothering me, Sally, and I just wanted to get it off my chest. About Landsman's will, of course. It seems pretty apparent, looking through these notes again, that he really was going to change the beneficiaries, although I have no idea why."

"You don't give up, do you, Adam Chauncey?"

"You've got me there, but one puzzle solved, maybe! Even if it leads to another."

"So what are you going to do? And how will you ever know if there's any legal record of what he intended?"

"Maybe he died before he could change his will. But I think there are two things we need to find out. One is to confirm the identity of those people whose names he listed. And secondly, we need to find out if he had told anyone at the firm that he was contemplating a change. And maybe, if we do another more careful search of his apartment, we'll find a second will."

"How will you determine if he consulted anyone? You can't just barge into every partner's office and ask."

"There's Bill Evans. We could talk to him again."

"Maybe, and maybe he'll just choose to hide out again in a fog."

"Or if he did contact anyone at Smithson and Dwyer, there's got to be a record of it: an appointment, even a phone call."

"So you're planning on charming the partners' receptionist. Get him to open all the records for you, just like that."

"No," Adam said. "I'm thinking you could do it, Sally. I don't think I'd be successful."

"Unless he's gay. Have you thought of that?"

"I doubt it. Anyway, it would look less suspicious . . . less important if you were just confirming some last-minute information for me."

"Not sure what I'd tell him."

"You'll think of something, Sally."

"Well, not this late at night. I'll talk to you tomorrow," she said and hung up.

Chapter 6

Adam arrived early the next morning, just as the cleaning crew was packing up their mops and buckets to leave. It was always a clumsy moment when he encountered one of the workers inside his office. They were usually Latino, although it never seemed to be the same person, and he inevitably stumbled in his greeting, not knowing if he should address them in his limited Spanish, assuming that this was their first language, or English so as not to stereotype them. Just friendly, the way he actually felt, was best. Nonetheless, it was always surprising to find an intruder there, and it sometimes made him picture what it might be like if he had been a cleaner, dusting and tidying one of the lavish offices of the partners on the upper floor. He could picture himself sitting back for a moment in someone's comfortable leather chair, putting his feet up on the desk, and barking out orders to an imaginary secretary, taking down every word while he or she glanced up at him in awe. But no one would think to do that in his cinderblock workplace with its confusion of papers, bare walls, and untidy conference table.

So he just said hello as the cleaner stepped out of the door. Hanging up his coat, he sat down on his own uncomfortable chair and stared at the pile of files that he had pulled out of his briefcase. There was still the puzzle of what they meant. Puzzles, plural, because he wasn't sure what they suggested (what Landsman intended) or whom the names represented—the Sanchezes, one woman and two children perhaps— and their relationship to him. How would he ever be able to find them if, presumably, he actually tried? And there was the larger question of whether he should be concerned at all. Maybe Sally was right: it might be best just to get on with the probate and distributions and let these strange scraps of unknown intention remain just that—odds and ends of what might have been mere second thoughts. Just stick to the letter of the law, he told himself. Keep your head down and do what was expected of you.

He was startled out of this contemplation by a knock at the door. Getting half out of his chair, he watched as Sally breezed in, fresh and prim and, he noticed, looking particularly elegant this morning.

"I've been thinking," she began. "Thought about this last night after I got home and talked to you. Of course, you don't have to do anything I suggest. But I've changed my mind. I think your initial impression was right. I think our Mr. Landsman was contemplating a new will. And those new names were certainly to be the beneficiaries. The only question is how far he got. If he spoke to one of the partners, if there was a new will in the works, I think we ought to find out."

"Sit down, Sally, and let's try to figure out, if you're right, what we should do. At a minimum, I suppose we could find out if Landsman contacted anyone here at the firm about a new will—and if there was even a draft. And why, if there is one, that no one has mentioned it. And then, we can go back to his office and do a more thorough search. I'm sorry we didn't finish it yesterday when we had the chance. But I wasn't convinced these were more than random notes to himself." He looked intently at her. "And I know. I'm getting ahead of myself here, suggesting there might be some sort of conspiracy of silence upstairs. Certainly have no evidence whatsoever of that or why there might be one."

"But you want to find out, don't you, Adam?"

"You're damned right. So are you willing to do what I suggested? Try to find out if Landsman had a recent appointment with someone upstairs. Charm that officious door supervisor and gentleman bouncer in the partners' lobby."

"I'll try my best."

"And I'm sure that will be more than enough!"

She laughed and said, "Wish me luck. I'll go now before things get too hectic up there."

Adam smiled to himself as she left the room and closed the door firmly behind her. If anyone could pry information out of that pompous sentry, he was certain that she could.

Ten minutes later, Sally emerged from the elevator and walked into the partners' lobby. Ted Smith took a moment to look up from whatever he was reading on his desk. No doubt, she thought, this was a studied hesitation to make any visitor feel diminished and unimportant, a supplicant for his attention.

"May I help you?" he finally said, flashing a brief smile.

"Yes, you may. I'm Sally Warren from the paralegal department downstairs. I need some information to complete the filing of a will that my supervisor is the executor of. Very simple."

"Of course, Miss Warren. Just let me know what it is, and I'll decide if I can accommodate you."

Sally hesitated for a moment and then approached closer to the desk. "Do you mind if I sit here?" she said, sinking down into the chair beside his desk and crossing her legs.

An uncomfortable look passed over his face as he watched her.

"Sure," he said after a moment. "Please yourself. Now, what is it that you want."

"It's just a small detail, and I know that you're the right person to find it for me."

"I'll try . . . if, of course, it isn't privileged information."

"I'm sure you will be the best judge of that," she said, smiling.

He looked away for a moment and then returned to stare at her.

"It concerns the will of Percy Landsman. My senior, Mr. Adam Chauncey—I'm sure you know of him—he's the executor, and we're just clearing up a few loose ends before we go to probate."

"I suppose I've heard of him, yes. Of course, I can't be sure. There's such a crowd of juniors. Hard to keep track of them."

Sally offered him an indulgent smile as if the two of them shared some secret confidence. "Yes, it must be a rather difficult task you have. I don't envy you keeping track of everything. I'm sure it takes considerable efficiency."

"Yes," he said.

"But what I need is just a tidbit of information. Mr. Chauncey wants to know if Landsman had a recent appointment here."

"I'm not sure that I can divulge that if he did stop in."

"I can certainly understand your hesitation. I think it's admirable to be cautious. You are certainly right. But, you see, there is something unclear in the will, and the original partner who's the prime executor is ill and unable to provide any clarification. So if Mr. Landsman came in any time before his death, well, we need to know if he consulted with anyone else on the off chance that he explained his intentions better. So we can proceed."

"I'm not sure," Smith said. "It's a bit unusual."

Leaning forward and fiddling with the top button of her blouse, Sally said, "But you'll make the right decision, of course. I trust your judgment."

"Let me look up recent appointments," he said after a moment. "And if I find anything, I'll ask one of the partners if I can convey that information to you."

"That would be splendid," she said. "I'll just wait, if you don't mind."

"Well, I suppose I could look at the schedule . . . let you know if there was an appointment. I don't see the harm in that."

"Perfect, and then you can ask whoever it was with if there was anything substantial that we need to know. I was certain you would think of a solution."

She leaned back in her chair, and Smith turned away to look at his desktop. It took several minutes as he called up the appointment schedule on his computer and scrolled through the last several months' dates. Finally, he stopped and then turned back to face her.

"You're in luck. It appears that Mr. Landsman did make an appointment just about six weeks ago with Mr. Emsback. I have no information as to whether he actually appeared. You know, sometimes clients are callous about their obligations. And frankly, I don't remember."

"I'm sure that makes your job very difficult. The partners must really appreciate you!"

"Yes, I suppose they do. Anyway, I'll find out if he appeared and if anything of substance was discussed. I can let you know, Miss Warren."

"Thank you so much," she said. "I was certain that you would be helpful." She sat for a minute more and then rose to leave. "You can call me anytime," she said as she walked out to the hallway and the elevator bank, very conscious that he was watching her.

Back in Adam's office, sitting at the conference table, Sally reported the gist of her brief conversation: "Landsman did make an appointment a while ago—I don't know the exact date. I didn't ask because I didn't want to appear too anxious. And it isn't certain that he actually kept the rendezvous. Apparently, with Mr. Emsback. That's all that I was privileged to know. But I'm sure that the receptionist will consult with the partner, and he promised to get back to me."

"I knew you'd find out something, Sally," Adam said. "You could charm the birds out of the trees."

"More like a snake charmer in this case," Sally said. "You know how protective people like that can be. The butler's always more of a snob than the gentles he serves."

Adam chuckled and shook his head. "No doubt. But the important thing is that we weren't wrong to follow up on that file. Something was obviously bothering Landsman."

"Yes, but what? It could have been anything."

"If he did come in and your confidant upstairs runs to one of the partners—as I suspect he will—then I'm pretty sure we'll hear something else. Of course, it could have been a no-show appointment. Remember that Landsman was probably feeling very ill at the time, maybe too sick to come in. Or perhaps it was something entirely else and inconsequential, and we'll never know. Or maybe we're kicking the hornets' nest."

"So what should we do now? What are you going to do about probate?"

"Nothing yet. Let's just wait on that. Until this is all cleared up. And maybe we can find out something about the names on Landsman's scribblings. Sanchez, right?"

"But how in the world? There must be a thousand people named Sanchez in Chicago and countless more nationally. My god, we'd never find out."

"I don't know, Sally. Honestly, I'm stumped. Of course, we have their first initials, too, and that might be a start. But I have no idea what their relationship to him might have been. For all we know, it could relate to some business association."

"I don't think you put that kind of person in a will—at least not that kind of partner."

"So you agree it's got to be someone closer? But no relation to his former wife. She was named Taylor, right? So it must be the family he mentioned in the letter attached to his will."

"Relationships don't always occur downstream," Sally said.

"What in the world does that mean?"

"I suppose that since he was adopted, he must have found out the name of his birth mother. Someone named Sanchez."

Adam looked intently at her. "OK. That's certainly plausible. Proof of why I keep you around, Sally."

"And all the while, I thought it was my good looks and clever conversation," she replied.

"That too. That too. Except that now you've posed an even greater problem. How do we ever locate his birth mother, if it was always Sanchez or something else prior? Maybe she got married and changed it to Sanchez."

"But that isn't likely. You told me she died in childbirth."

"If that's true," he replied. "But I'm starting to doubt everything I've heard about this situation. So I say we have to go back to his flat and examine his papers again and see if we can find out if he was investigating his ancestry. It's pretty obvious that he found something."

"Or we could ask Eric Landsman if he remembers the name of their maid—find her that way. Except . . ."

"Yes?"

"Except that I don't want anyone to know quite yet what we're doing. And anyway, I don't know what it would tell us. Just another name."

"You're right. It's a long shot, but I don't see any other way to begin except to find out if we missed something in his papers. But . . ." she hesitated, "I think you need to stop just a second, Adam. Consider the consequences. Are you sure you want to pursue this? It might lead to trouble for you here at the firm."

"I suppose it might. But think of how we'd feel—how I'd feel—if we didn't follow this up. I mean, just to be sure."

As he spoke, there was the sound of a text message arriving on his desktop.

"I'd better see what that is," he said, clicking the mouse.

He looked at the screen for a moment and then said, "They want to see me upstairs. One of the partners, Frank Emsback, who wrote the original will. Wow! That was quick! Let me read the message: 'Could you please come to my office this afternoon around two for a brief conference? I have a few matters to discuss with you."

"Short and to the point."

"But not so insistent that he's willing to miss lunch."

"Can't argue with you there, so maybe it's nothing."

"Yes, except that you and I know both know it's the result of your inquiry into Landsman's appointment."

"Then we'll have to postpone our search of his townhouse until tomorrow."

"I suppose that can wait," he said.

"And anyway, I scheduled the movers to come next week and the cleaners after that," she said. "So everything can just stew for a day or two more."

Adam laughed. "I'm not sure I like that metaphor. Makes me think there's going to be a fire under our investigation."

"There is," she said, "and you're holding the match. So watch out and don't burn your fingers. And in the meantime, I've got to get back to the paralegal pen. I'm sure they're missing me."

"But if you go, then I'll be missing you," he said.

Sally looked at him, stood up, and retreated to the doorway. "Be careful while I'm gone, Mr. Junior Associate Chauncey."

After a quick trip to the café takeout kiosk in the building, Adam returned to his office, sat down, and removed the lunch he had purchased from the paper bag, spreading the contents on the desk: a sad-looking chicken salad sandwich on soggy white bread with the crusts snipped off, a bag of chips that he knew would make him thirsty, and a can of Coke that would only make him thirstier. He realized that this was all bad for him, that it would rev up his excitement with a burst of empty energy and then dump him down exhausted. He knew he had to stop eating junk, but he didn't have the time or inclination to pack a lunch in the early morning, and a restaurant was out of the question. He had too much work to do.

He took a few bites of the sandwich and shoved it back in the plastic wrap and tipped it into the trash can. Wiping his greasy fingers on the paper napkin that came with it, he clicked the computer mouse and scrolled down to open the brief that had been handed to him two days before—something he was responsible to examine but had put off until now. Busy work was always slogged off on the juniors, he thought.

"I wonder when they'll replace us with robots and processing units," he said out loud. "Won't be long before they pull up the ladder and let us all sink."

"And," he added, "look who's feeling sorry for themselves just because of a rotten lunch!"

Just before two o'clock, he stepped out of the elevator and walked into the partners' lobby. As usual, Ted Smith was sitting behind his desk, head bowed and apparently preoccupied. Glancing up at the interruption, he motioned for Adam to sit down. "Wait," he said and resumed whatever urgent app on his cell phone was commanding his attention. But he looked up when Adam continued walking up to the desk.

"I have an appointment with Mr. Emsback. Would you please let him know I'm here?"

Smith seemed slightly confused by Adam's small breach of etiquette, as if he realized that his own status and power depended entirely on his ability to make someone wait. With a quick furtive motion, he put away his phone.

"Of course," he mumbled. "If you don't mind sitting for a moment, I'll let him know you're here."

Adam stepped away but remained standing in the middle of the room.

After a brief, muffled conversation, Smith hung up the intercom phone and stood up slightly. "Just a minute, please," he said, smiling. "Please sit down, and I'll let you know when he's available."

Adam recognized the charade, wondering if the receptionist had actually phoned the partner or if this was his way of re-establishing his authority. *Damn the formality of this place*, he thought.

He sat down and waited almost ten minutes before Smith signaled to him. "He's coming out," he said without looking up.

As he said this, the door opened, and Emsback emerged from the corridor that led to a bank of offices. Spotting Adam, he walked over briskly, extended his hand, and gripped Adam's firmly.

"Glad you could make it," he said. "And sorry about the small delay. But you know."

Adam had a minute to study him before he turned and led the way back toward his office. Emsback just looked lawyer all over. He was not the sort of smiling, slightly seedy TV mouthpiece flashing overactive optimism and promising a huge payoff for pain and suffering, but a man about whom one could only utter the word *distinguished*. He was about Adam's height, wearing a dark pin-striped suit with a deep-red tie. His face was slightly flushed, the color coming either from a weekend vacation or some outdoor activity; his entirely white hair was long and full. The perfectly etched earnest lines on his face seemed to indicate complete sincerity and trustworthiness, and there was his decisive stride. Adam was puzzled that such a manicured appearance could also seem slightly menacing. Perhaps it was just too studied.

The door to his office was ajar. Adam followed him inside, and they sat, across from each other in a corner conversation area on dark leather couches.

Apparently in no hurry to begin, Emsback allowed Adam a moment to look around the room. It was dark-wood paneled—oak or walnut perhaps—with one large window that looked out at the gray-and-silver skyline and, perhaps, below where he couldn't see, onto a slim margin of the Chicago River. On the wall behind the large desk, there were a number of framed photographs. Adam couldn't make out the faces, but the setting in each seemed to be a golf course. On the desk to the right was a computer terminal, and to the left was a brass statue of a golfer in mid-swing. Some kind of trophy. Unlike the clutter of his own workspace, this sparse and elegant order had the swagger of confidence and success.

"I see you're looking at the photos. You can look at them up close if you want. They're my pride—one with Tiger and the other with Jack Nicklaus. Do you ever play? Lots of wonderful courses in the area."

"I've never really tried, sir," Adam said.

"Please, it's Frank. Well, now, we'll have to get you out on the links one of these days. I'm not promising I could teach you anything. Something of a duffer myself. But you could take some lessons. Several of the partners belong to Sunset Ridge near Winnetka. I think it's the best course around. Membership by invitation only, of course, but naturally, with such close ties to the firm, and we could put in a good word. Of course, there are other courses in the area if you're so inclined, but we like to think of Sunset as our own private club. You know," he confided, "that way, the only surprises are a bad lie in the rough!"

"Sounds like a great place," Adam said, trying to sound interested. "I'll certainly think about it."

Emsback studied him for a moment, pausing too long, and then said, finally, "Are you happy here, Mr. Chauncey . . . Adam? Are we keeping you busy? I know that being a junior is pretty difficult and boring—hard to see your way into a future partnership. I can remember those days, myself. But if you work hard and successfully, you'll find yourself up here with the rest of us in no time."

"I do enjoy my work, sir. And I certainly like the law. No complaints at all."

"And how about the paralegals? How do you find them? Helpful?"

"Very helpful, very competent."

"That's good. Because I might be asking you for your advice about one or two of them in the future. You know we sometimes select one to bring on as an associate."

"I'll certainly keep my eyes open."

"Well, I think that's all," Emsback said, standing. "Except I want you to look at my pictures up close. They're my pride."

Adam stood and walked over to the wall behind the desk. Indeed, it was true. There were two shots of Emsback standing next to a grinning Tiger Woods and Jack Nicklaus. Both were autographed.

"Very impressive," he said. "You must take the game very seriously."

"Second only to the law, despite my handicap," Emsback said.

"Well," Adam said after he looked at the pictures again, "I think I'd better go back to work. I appreciate our conversation, sir. And I will think about the golf."

"Good boy," Emsback said with a lingering grip on his shoulder. "That's the winning attitude. And don't let yourself get distracted. Just let the firm do your thinking for you."

Adam walked out of the room, past the receptionist, who gave him an interested look, and then rode the elevator back down to his office. Sally was sitting at the conference table, a cup of coffee and some papers in front of her. She looked up as he entered.

"Well," she said. "Was it a warning?"

"I'm not sure," he replied, sitting down across from her. "Not a single word about the will or Landsman or anything substantial."

"So what was it about?"

"Mainly temptation," Adam replied. "And something about a golf course."

"That must be a relief."

"Unless you don't play golf. But why the sudden attention and a meeting about nothing?"

"They must think you're a prodigy."

"Or someone to keep a cautious eye on."

Late that evening, Adam sat on the couch of his small living room, a half-empty glass of beer next to the smeared pizza box on the table in front of him. A muted television show flickered blue shadows around the room, highlighting the bookshelf behind him, a desk and chair, and a cabinet where several framed pictures were set up on top, the faces indistinct in the dancing light. He reached for his cell phone and then tossed it back down again without looking at the screen. The idea of calling Sally this late or any evening again was a bad impulse he needed to resist. He would see her soon enough—tomorrow—and he wasn't sure what he wanted to say in any case; perhaps he was looking for reassurance. At least he knew better than to share his ugly mood. He realized that his sour disposition was a hangover from his meeting with Emsback, and the more he thought about it, the less he liked that man with his choreographed manners. And he also regretted being less than honest with Sally. It had been a warning, clearly so. A veiled threat dressed up as an invitation to play golf that he knew wasn't serious. And the warning wasn't just aimed at him but at her too—that odd mention of paralegals. Yes, he certainly got the message.

The only question now was, should he continue to question the Landsman will or not? It was clear that there were eyes on him. It could all be innocent enough. After all, this was a large fortune, and he was the executor—for the first time. But how to explain the anomalies of the will—that addendum about Landsman's family? And the notes about different beneficiaries. And there was Emsback's warning. If anything, it all made him even more suspicious that something was wrong.

In moments like this, he couldn't stop himself from revisiting all the decisions that had led him upstate to Chicago and the firm. True enough, leaving Southern Illinois had been the easiest choice to make. His childhood had been happy enough, although meandering from one interest and hobby to the next. His mother, Dora, was too preoccupied with herself, trying to keep up appearances on the meager wages of a schoolteacher, to offer much guidance. Because he was an unruly boy, prone to sudden excitements and rebellious to every one of her efforts to "civilize" him, as she sometimes put it, she tended to ignore him. All her advice, if you could call it that, was to see the rosy side of every situation. But behind her careful façade of cheerfulness and "making do" early on, he had sensed something desperate and bitter as if she blamed her husband for his early death, for marooning her in widowhood and the solitary role of an aging, single mother. Adam was painfully aware that all his friends had fathers, and he alone was without the bragging rights and companionship that they possessed. He was acutely aware of just how much their conversations were inflected with boasts about their families. There were even moments when he envied the stern and sometimes unjust punishments meted out by these disciplinarians that his friends complained about. In contrast, his mother never said a word except to urge him always to make the best of things. You could almost hate someone who met every adversity in a slush of sentimental nonsense. Perhaps that is what convinced him that skepticism and realism were pretty much the same thing.

So leaving home had been easy and inevitable, despite the occasional twinge of guilt he felt, knowing that he was visiting a second abandonment on her. At university, upstate, he floundered for the first two years, taking a smorgasbord of courses, doing well enough, but mindful that he felt no excitement or anticipation glancing through the windows of enlightenment that were being opened to him. Looking back now, he guessed that one reason might be guilt for leaving, for inventing a new existence that he felt he could never really share with his mother. But that feeling had finally passed, and the one subject that attracted him—the units devoted to the law in his political science courses—gave him a new sense of direction. Yes, that was the best way to describe the feeling. It was the experience of something concrete, real, and substantial—philosophical debates over tangible and important issues. He had drifted along until he bumped up against what he felt was firm and stationary for the first time in his life. He had needed no encouragement to clamber aboard.

Perhaps it was pent-up enthusiasm that allowed him to excel in law school and easily pass his boards. But it was pure chance that he was hired by Smithson and Dwyer. He always thought and still considered it an accidental convergence of something he must have said at the interview and the receptivity of the partner who had a line-up of twenty young and eager women and men (among them some legacy applicants bearing the names of the city's founding elites) waiting anxiously outside the door of that hotel room in Chicago—some chance trigger that he had inadvertently released. Something inexplicable. In fact, he could hardly believe his good luck if that was what it was. And now, he found himself at the bottom of the firm, looking up toward a partnership among a pack of hustling associates, several of whom he knew would never squeeze through the narrow door of promotion. And despite his better sense and the insistent voice of ambition, here he was making trouble over the simple execution of an undisputed will.

For all of his introspection, there was a lot he just didn't understand about himself. He thought he wanted, more than anything, to become a partner in the firm, to walk into his own luxurious office on the upper floor, to pass by that mincing receptionist allowing him only a shrug of recognition, to have an exclusive membership in the club. Maybe learn golf. Yet some contrary compulsion was pushing him to sabotage that ambition, some gnawing dissatisfaction that would surely endanger his position. Maybe he was just stubborn. Or maybe it was his tendency to feel the opposite of what he was told. But one thing was sure: he did regret lying to Sally. There was no doubt in his mind that the conference with Frank Emsback had been a warning: a clenched fist in a velvet glove. The partner had laid out before him the future that would surely be snatched away if he persisted. And he was pretty sure that the simple inquiry to the receptionist about Landsman's visit had touched off a flurry of concern upstairs. He wondered if it was too late to turn back now. Maybe he had already closed that narrow door of his future.

He woke the next morning with the recognition that sleep had resolved nothing—not even the fatigue he felt. He sat in his small kitchen alcove with a cup of black coffee, squinting to read the unpronounceable ingredients in small print on the box of cereal in front of him. The window over his right shoulder was just a patch of gray that was too weak to light the room. When he turned to look outside, he could only see the bare latticework of the tree next to his apartment. It looked cold outside, even if it wasn't—the way spring in Chicago sometimes put on a menacing appearance as if it begrudged the summer to come.

He stood up reluctantly, straightened his tie, and looked at the weather app on his cell phone. "Cloudy with showers and seasonal." Whatever that meant! He grabbed a coat for his walk to the "L" and the short trip to the office.

He was one of the first to arrive, and he took the time to arrange the confusion on his desk and turn on his desktop to see if there were any messages or new assignments that had come through during the evening. He had left the door open so that Sally would know he was waiting to talk to her.

Shortly after nine, she appeared at the entrance and knocked firmly.

"Come on in, Sally," he said, looking up.

Entering halfway, she looked at him quizzically. "Bad night?" she asked.

"Does it show, then?"

"Something does."

"Maybe you're just seeing indecision. Come on in and sit down."

When she had settled onto a chair at the conference table, he walked over and joined her. "I've been thinking about this will thing again. I've half a mind to let everything drop and get on with it."

"And what does your better half say?"

He laughed. "Well, it says, 'Continue on no matter what the consequences.'"

"And do you know which half will prevail?"

"I don't know, Sally. What do you think? I have to confess, I'm sure now that I was being warned to lay off yesterday. It's no coincidence that I got called upstairs for a conference. The message was clear enough."

"And . . ."

"I understand, but it's made me really curious. I guess you know how I react to veiled threats."

"I do now," she said.

"So I think we should do a bit more research. Just find out if Landsman was going to change his will and name different beneficiaries. Because even if that's true, there's nothing to be done. No new will."

"So it's only curiosity?"

"Yes, and wondering why the upstairs is trying to caution me."

"So what now?"

"Why don't you grab your coat, Sally? Let's take another trip back to Landsman's apartment, do a more thorough search, and see if there's anything else in his papers. Last time, we just skimmed the surface, didn't know what we were looking for."

"And now we do?" she said, standing up and walking to the door.

"Maybe."

As he watched her disappear, Adam noticed for the first time that she was wearing slacks and a sweater, almost as if she had expected that she needed to dress for something more strenuous than a day staring at her desktop. He couldn't help but smile.

The day had brightened considerably when they finally found a parking place a couple of blocks beyond Landsman's apartment. But a brisk, chilly wind had come whipping up off the lake. *Chicago spring gives and then takes back*, Adam thought as they mounted the steps to the townhouse.

As soon as they entered, both of them quickly realized that something fundamental had changed. All of the furniture downstairs had been removed, leaving only depressions in the living room carpet where a couch and tables had once rested; there were grimy outlines on the walls where a few pictures had hung.

Walking into the kitchen through the empty dining room, Sally began pulling out drawers and opening cabinets.

"It's all gone," she exclaimed. "Everything. Every last cup and saucer. There's obviously been some mistake because I arranged with the removers to come next week, not yesterday. Somehow they got the date wrong."

Adam said nothing but turned and bounded up the stairs, taking the last two steps in one stride. He hurried straight to the empty office and stood in the doorway. Turning to Sally, who was coming up behind him, he almost shouted, "It's all gone. All his papers, everything. The only thing they left is the dust!"

Sally squeezed by him to look. "It's a disaster," she said. "What now?"

"We'll have to call the removal company immediately and see if they still have his documents. Do you have their number on your cell?"

"No, I'm afraid it's in my files back in the office."

"OK, then, let's go. No reason to stay here a minute longer." He didn't add that this couldn't have been a mistake. Someone had ordered this unscheduled clean-up. But who would do such a thing and why? He was reluctant to say anything, even if he was sure he knew.

When they reached Sally's car, she hesitated at the door. "You drive, Adam. I'm really nervous, and I don't trust myself in traffic."

"I'd trust you anywhere, Sally," he said. "But give me the keys. I'll try to get us back downtown in one piece."

She smiled and handed him the fob.

Neither of them said much on the trip back to the parking lot under the building next to the office, but Adam was sure that they were thinking much the same thing—or better, wondering how the mix-up of moving dates had occurred, except that it probably wasn't a mix-up. This muddle of possibilities reminded him of the one thing he had never truly experienced during his sentimental childhood, where his mother could only see the bright side of adversity and certainly never admitted to anyone's hostile intentions. As a result, he had never really learned when exactly to be suspicious. The irony was that law was all about guarding against unseemly motives, and every contract he drew up or brief that the firm sent him had to parry every possible angle of deception or hidden advantage. That was the essence of the profession he had chosen—and he had learned it well. And now that he thought about it, perhaps this unfamiliar world of mistrust was another of its attractions for him. But there was still something deep down inside him that made him reluctant to doubt anyone's good intentions. He was still his mother's son. Of course, he might say out loud that he had suspicions, but somehow his reluctance to distrust never seemed to match the words he might utter. And now he was torn between wondering if someone was meddling with Landsman's legacy or the increasingly unlikely event of a simple mistake. But who would do that and why? He was sure he didn't want to know.

Back in his office, he waited for Sally while she looked up the number of the disposal company. Glancing at his emails and then at the pile of unfinished work on his desk, he knew that he was running behind the tight schedule that all the associates were on. The Landsman case—he stopped abruptly and realized that he had thought the word *case* as if to designate this as something deeply troubling and unresolved. But increasingly, he knew it was. There was something not right about it. And what had at first seemed a loose end that needed a quick tie-up was now becoming more serious. He was beginning to *feel* that something was seriously amiss.

"I've got the information," Sally said, rushing into the room. "At least this is the company we hired a while back." She handed him a slip of paper. He took it and dialed the number.

Sally listened intently to his half of the conversation. When he finished, he put the receiver firmly back in the cradle.

"Damn it," he said. "All they could give me was the contact and address of the disposal company and a storage facility. No explanation for the change of dates or who ordered it."

"So what should we do now?"

"I guess we get in your car again and drive to where they've taken his things. No point in calling them first. We need to go right now."

"Where is it?" she asked.

"Some commercial warehouse, West Side, out near Cicero."

"You'll drive again?"

"Yes, if you want me to."

"I do."

On the highway going west, the traffic was jammed up with early rush-hour commuters.

"I couldn't do this every day," Sally said, "I'd be weaving in and out, honking my horn, giving people the finger."

"Or you could just make your car your home away from home," Adam said. "You know, text your friends, drink a cup of coffee, maybe a bag of chips sitting on the passenger seat, put on or take off make-up, listen to some talk show like everyone else."

"Do you really think that's me?"

"No."

She was silent for a moment. "Adam, I'm worried that the storage place might be closed. Maybe we should have called first."

"We'll probably just make it," he said. "It's not far, and it's only four o'clock. Can't imagine they have bankers' hours."

"Or partners'!"

He said nothing but continued on until they reached the turn-off at Route 50 and then reversed back several blocks.

The building they approached was a massive, geometric structure, the shape of an engineer's clipboard, three or four stories high, windowless, with some sort of opaque yellow cladding. The bulk of it stood on pillars, creating a space high enough to allow trucks to enter and unload underneath. From what they could see as they drove around it, the surface took up almost two consecutive city blocks, with additional large space for parking in front.

Adam stopped the car as close as possible, and together, they walked out and halfway around the building until they found the glass doors of the entrance. It wasn't what they expected. Inside was an empty lobby with a bank of elevators on the right, a door leading to a hallway, and a large directory and blueprint indicating the location of several businesses.

"I think it's some sort of merchandise mart," Sally exclaimed as she examined the floorplan. "Like a discount mall or maybe a shipping terminal for downtown department stores . . . furniture, clothing."

"Do you see the storage company?"

"Yes," she said. "Here it is. Through the doorway and about halfway down on this floor."

"Let's go, then," he said, pushing through and then, at the last second, remembering to hold the door for her.

They walked quickly down the brightly lighted hallway, passing by two glass entranceways to what looked like showrooms until they reached the storage company entrance.

Stepping inside, they entered a small reception area, empty except for a high metallic desk and a metal door to its right, with nothing visible through the small wired glass window in the top half.

Adam walked closer to the desk and found a call bell. He pressed it, and they waited.

After a minute or so, the door opened, and a very short woman dressed in a dark-blue jumpsuit entered. She disappeared behind the desk and then reappeared, apparently mounting onto some sort of stool or steps behind it. She leaned over the top and looked at them, smiling briefly.

"What can I do for you two?" she asked.

"Yes," Adam said. "I represent the law firm of Smithson and Dwyer. I'm the executor of the estate of a Mr. Percy Landsman, and I believe that his belongings have been sent here for storage. We're here to examine the contents."

The woman looked puzzled, and she hesitated for a moment to twist a strand of hair back into place:

"That's real strange," she said. "I wouldn't know anything about it excepting that the shipment arrived only yesterday evening very late. Special order. Usually, things just sit around for ages like nobody knows they're here until we get an instruction to junk them. You'd be surprised about the things people are thinking they want to keep—just stuff—and then forget. But now yous two."

"I know it's unusual, but . . ."

"And I don't know nothing about no law firm. It was the disposal company that contacted us—far as I remember. Nothing about no lawyers, except I guess that lawyers slither out from every rock you turn over these days, like. You see 'em on the television ads all the time. Anyways, I got to check the paperwork and talk to the boss to see if they'll let you in. Probably not. Don't get your hopes up."

She stepped down and then walked back through the door and disappeared.

Sally looked at Adam nervously.

"I wish there was some place to sit down," she said.

"Cerberus," he replied.

"What?" she said, giving him a strange look.

"You know, the dog . . . Cerberus."

"No, I don't, Adam. And I don't know Latin either."

"It's the dog, the hound of Hades. And from the Greek myth."

"But what are you talking about?"

"She made me think of the dog that guards the gates to hell."

"I don't know about you sometimes, Adam," she laughed. "Where did that come from?"

"My distant Southern Illinois past and my mother's legacy, I guess. I think I told you she was a schoolteacher and always anxious about the proper things to learn and know. So I had to take a Latin course in high school. And one of our first assignments was to learn the names of Greek gods. Turned out to be one of the most embarrassing moments of my teenage years because I was the only boy in the class. Got teased a lot because of it. Of course, now that I look back on it, it just seems like a lost opportunity."

"Huh?"

"All those girls, I mean. Anyway, our Cerberus here is looking for a reason not to let us in."

"But why would she?"

"Probably her first instinct is to say no. Then when she finally agrees, we'll feel obligated. That's the first rule of a bureaucracy, isn't it? Place the customer at a disadvantage, and when she grudgingly agrees to whatever it is we're asking, we'll feel grateful. Puts us on the wrong foot, to begin with."

"That's a little complicated, Adam."

He was about to respond when the door opened and the woman reappeared, this time carrying a sheath of papers that she placed on the desk.

"The boss says you can come on in," she said. "But you got to sign this release. Then I'll take you back."

Adam picked up the paper, scribbled his name next to an X at the bottom of the final sheet, and handed it to the woman.

"Really strange that this shipment just arrived yesterday and then you arriving just like that. Like I say, folks usually just dump stuff and forget about it."

She turned without another word and opened the hallway door.

She led them down a dimly lit corridor past several wire cage enclosures, some with stacks of furniture and appliances, others piled high with boxes and crates. Toward the very end, she stopped in front of a large storage space and unlocked the gate. Adam recognized some of Landsman's furniture.

"I'll leave you here," the woman said. "Don't have much time 'cause we're closing up soon. If you finish early, just push that buzzer." She indicated a metal utility box with a red button attached to the side of the enclosure. "Otherwise, I'll come bring you out."

"Thanks very much for your help, Miss . . . ?" Adam said.

"It's Mrs. . . . Mrs. Nubbin." She turned away and disappeared.

Sally looked at Adam, shook her head slightly, and then walked into the storage space.

"I guess we need to find his desk and maybe his papers if they boxed them up separately."

"Right, Sally. I think that's the desk over there. Why don't you see if any of those boxes are labeled?"

For the next ten minutes, they opened drawers and looked inside every box. It was hot work, and they were both sweating when Adam finally said, "They're not here. Not a scrap of paper anywhere. And the computer is missing too. I think we need to talk to our gatekeeper right away. Maybe she knows where the files are."

He walked over to the outside wall and pressed the buzzer. After a minute or so, Mrs. Nubbin appeared.

"What's the problem? You done already?" she asked as she entered the storage area.

"The papers and files. They're all missing. Do you know where they are?"

"Yep," she replied. "But you didn't ask about them."

"I know, I know," Adam said. "We just assumed they'd be here with everything else. So where are they?"

"Disposal unit."

"My god!" said Sally.

"Ready for recycling, I'd guess."

"But we need to see them immediately," Adam exclaimed. "Can you take us there? It's very important. These are valuable documents."

"Don't know about that. Far as I know, there's an order to destroy them. Standard practice. Not sure I can do anything."

"Can't you speak to your supervisor?" Adam asked, trying very hard not to show his anger. "I'm sure there's been some mistake. We need those documents for legal purposes." He stressed the word *legal*.

"I'll see. But you know it's getting late. He may have went home by now. Why didn't you come earlier if it was so important?"

Adam just shook his head as Mrs. Nubbin left them again.

"I don't like this, Sally," he said. "As far as I know, there were never any instructions to destroy his papers unless you did, and I know you didn't. I certainly didn't anticipate that. And this hasty removal? All this has to be one of the partners."

"You're right. Has to be someone else at the firm—who else? Not me, for sure. And I'm exhausted. I think I'll sit down for a moment," she said as she pulled a chair off a pile of furniture and set it upright.

Adam remained standing. As he looked down at Sally, he could see a thin band of sweat on her forehead. Her face was flushed with a halo of energy from the exertion of moving boxes and furniture around. He thought she had never looked more seductive. And yes, there they were, alone and together, but not as he had imagined or wanted it in anxious intimacy, waiting in this dingy warehouse, rummaging through the disorderly remains of someone's life, someone that they had never met, searching for something that they didn't know existed or, if it did, whether they would recognize it. Hardly a romantic moment.

Almost ten minutes passed before Mrs. Nubbin reappeared.

"I got you some good news and bad," she said, a slow smile softening her stern features. "Some of them documents have already been destroyed. But the boss phoned down to disposal, and they're gonna hold off on the rest for you."

"Can you take us there?" Adam asked.

"Well, you couldn't find it yourselfs now, could you? Just follow on. And don't blame me if you get all covered with dust. I'm not going in with you, just to point the way."

"Sure," Adam said, walking out of the enclosure, "and thank you."

"Just a minute," she said. "Got to lock up. You'll have to hold on."

Sally looked at Adam. She was sure that he was thinking the same thing—that this woman was thoroughly enjoying her slow-motion assistance and exacting as much vexation as she could from the situation. Well, if it made her feel good . . . nonetheless, she was, in the end, someone they had to depend upon, no choice.

Their guide led them slowly back toward the entrance and to a door that neither of them had noticed before.

"In there," she said. "Foreman's the name of Burns, and he knows you're coming."

She turned away, and Adam twisted the heavy doorknob, and he and Sally entered a cavernous room. At the very center was a large industrial paper shredder, a jerry-built-looking contraption with a large metal belly on stilts, an attached ladder on the side, and a long, segmented chute. Next to the front of it was an immense pile of confetti—long, useless tendrils of chewed-up documents. Sitting at the other end were heaps of boxes waiting to be shredded. The atmosphere was stuffy, and despite the LED fixtures hanging from the ceiling, the room was obscured by clouds of hanging dust. As they entered, a tall, thin man wearing a blue jumpsuit—a version of Mrs. Nubbin's uniform—approached. His face was grimy, and his dark hair was speckled with tiny fragments of paper.

"You must be the party what wants them boxes of files from the estate that just come in. Too bad you're too late. Just started on 'em and got about halfway through. You can see here there are only three left. Boss tells me you can take 'em. Don't bother me none, just less work for me. And don't ask if it's possible to put anything back together. Some folks do. But see here," he said, bending over to grasp a handful of shredded paper, "just a fistful of nothing. You'd wear your eyes out just tryin'. What's done is done."

"We'll take what's remaining," Adam said. "Is there any way we can bring the car around to pick them up?"

"Sure. Loading dock just out that door over there. People get confused trying to find where this is from the outside, so I'll open up, and you can see it when you drive around. You'll be wanting to hurry. I clock out at five. Won't be here a minute after that."

Adam and Sally left quickly, walking down the long hallway, back to the lobby of the warehouse, and then out into the main building. By the time they reached the car, it was almost five, and Adam hopped into the driver's seat. He squealed the tires as he sped around the building. Neither of them had time to put on seatbelts, and the incessant dinging of the warning bell just added to the confusion of their hurry.

"I'm disoriented, so many twists and turns when we were walking inside that building. I have no idea where the loading dock is," Adam exclaimed.

"Just keep going. It's bound to be near here," Sally said. "There'll have to be a driveway or some sort of entrance. I'll see it. Just drive!"

"Counting on you, Sally," Adam said, glancing very briefly in her direction.

"There it is," she said suddenly. "Turn in right there!"

He braked and pulled into a wide space. Extending out from the building was a low platform and, beyond it, the open door.

They got out, and Adam opened the trunk. He could see that the three boxes had been shoved onto the outside edge. Vaulting up onto the raised area, he walked over and picked up the first box.

"It's not heavy," he said. "I'll hand it to you if you don't mind."

"I'm not sure, Adam," she said. "Is manual labor part of my job description now?"

He walked over to the edge and handed it down to her.

"Yes, duty number 5: 'Organize and archive all documents related to completed and ongoing cases.'"

"Yes, I remember now, but carrying boxes?"

"Duty number 6: 'Do whatever you're asked.'"

"Oh," she said, lifting the box from his hands, "I entirely forgot about that one!"

The trip back on the expressway to downtown Chicago was slow-moving on their side, but nothing to compare to the snarl of cars inching out from the Loop toward Oak Park and the suburbs beyond. Sally drove carefully, and as they approached the city, Adam said, "If you don't mind, could you drop me at my apartment? I know it's out of the way, but I don't want these boxes to lie around the office. Just to make sure."

"I understand," Sally said. "It's no bother. Just don't make this taxi service a habit."

He reminded her of the address and then said nothing for the remainder of the trip. He was afraid that if he gave voice to his suspicion that someone at the firm was interfering, it would be like confirming it as fact. And there was that word *suspicion* again. He was learning fast!

They were lucky to find a parking spot just in front of his apartment building.

"I'll take it from here," he said, opening the door and walking around to the trunk. He raised it and lugged the three boxes one by one up the steps of the building and then returned to stand at the driver's side of her car.

"I'll go through these tonight," he said, leaning into the open window. "If I find anything significant, I'll bring it to the office tomorrow. But I'm going to keep everything here just in case."

He reached inside and touched her shoulder. "You're a trooper, Sally. Can't thank you enough. I owe you a drink."

She looked up at him and shook her head. "Nope. You owe me a lot more than that, Mr. Adam Chauncey. Maybe you're not aware of it, but I'm risking my job by helping you out on your extracurricular investigation."

"If you're worried, I can always get someone else to help," he said, trying to sound as if he meant it.

"No. I'm on board till the end of this cruise. But I don't believe you've considered all the consequences."

He stepped back. "Not sure I want to know."

"Well, I think you should," she said, rolling up the window. "Tomorrow then."

He walked back to the front entrance of his building, opened it, and placed the boxes in the hallway. His flat was on the second floor, and he made three trips bringing in the papers. Throwing his coat on the couch in the living room, he was tempted to begin a search through the documents, but he realized that this was going to be a long night, and he was hungry.

If I start now, he thought, I'll just drink myself through the evening. It was better to damp down his excitement, eat something, and then begin a methodical search.

An hour later, after he had tossed out the paper tray from his microwave dinner and rinsed the knife and fork, he carried a half-full bottle of scotch and a glass into the study, where he had moved the three boxes. They lay in a neat stack holding the possibility of some answers to questions he hadn't formulated yet waiting for him.

He quickly realized that there was no particular order to what he and Sally had retrieved from the disposal center. Whoever had packed up Landsman's apartment was apparently in a hurry or just careless and tossed them in helter-skelter. Nothing was organized, mostly just jumbles of papers. He didn't know what he was looking for, so he had to examine everything carefully. But he thought he'd realize it if he found it. Maybe another will?

Toward midnight and to measure the sinking level of the bottle he had brought with him, having had more than enough to drink, he was ready to quit for the evening. The light from his desk lamp had begun to cast a fuzzy glow, and he was having trouble focusing. One more box to go, he thought. Hesitating, he reached down and opened the carton. It was much more than he had hoped for because he quickly realized that almost half the contents were various yearly diaries and datebooks. Something they had missed altogether. And if Landsman was a thorough record keeper, he'd have his life spelled out in appointments and reminders.

He reached in and picked up one journal at random. Thumbing through it quickly, he became almost angry at what he saw. Most of the entries were in some sort of shorthand. Not a code, exactly, but abbreviations and partial words. Nothing was going to be easy, he thought. And he would only become more frustrated if he tried to decipher anything tonight.

He stood up, clutching the edge of the desk to steady himself and stretched. He looked down at the confusion around him: the open cartons and discarded piles of paper scattered on the floor. Well, he thought, it was all slated for destruction anyway, no need for order. And then he noticed a manila file pressed against the interior of one of the boxes he had thought he had emptied. He hesitated: probably just more irrelevant paper. But the blur of alcohol and the late night hadn't entirely blunted his curiosity, so he leaned down and picked it out.

Opening it, he quickly recognized what it was: several sheets of what looked like the copy of a new will. He sat down immediately and turned to the last page to see if it had been signed and witnessed. That section was blank, so he turned back to the beginning, carefully noting every word. Ten minutes later, he had confirmed that everything was appropriately worded. The only difference between this document and the original will was a change in beneficiaries with very different amounts. There was a new heading simply listed as "the family of Maria Sanchez-Lopez," followed by several names. In his haste, Landsman had probably drawn up the document himself, which would account for the odd wording. And no executor was listed. That last detail didn't matter, of course. The court could appoint anyone for that function. But Adam wondered if it had ever been completed and then deposited with the firm—unless this was just a sketch of something that he was considering. The question was, did an executed will actually exist somewhere?

He didn't want to admit it, but now he understood why someone had ordered his papers destroyed. He knew he shouldn't make any hasty conclusions. Somewhere in the rest of this mess, there might be some credible explanation. But for what? He only knew that he would have to confront some very unpleasant, even dangerous, possibilities. He picked up the bottle and glass, switched off the light, and staggered into his bedroom.

Chapter 7

The next morning, he was late to arrive at the office. It seemed to be a recent habit, and worse, he couldn't quite remember how he had arrived—the subway, of course, but he had no recollection of the trip. Sitting down at his desk, he felt the anticipation of a bad headache—that fuzzy sensation and blurred vision that signaled oncoming pain. His sleep had been shallow and dreamless because he was semiconscious most of the night and troubled by nagging worries. The new will (even if he wasn't sure it was legal) hadn't been a complete surprise, but it presented immense complications. Although he had no evidence whatsoever that someone in the firm had intentionally and maliciously ordered the destruction of Landsman's documents, that now seemed a clear possibility, almost a sure thing. What bothered him in his sleepy conversations with himself were the doubts about what he was doing and discomfort with his growing recognition that his investigations would have disastrous implications for himself and perhaps for Sally too. Besides, for him to harbor misgivings seemed unnatural. Everything in his background instructed him to trust people, yet he found himself pursuing an inquiry into a perfectly legitimate will that had no troublesome complications. Everything about it had once appeared straightforward and above board. And now, here he was questioning the obvious and suspecting the partners of duplicity. And neglecting his other work besides.

When he looked up, he saw Sally standing at his half-open door.

"Please don't knock," he said, holding up his hand. "Just come in and sit for a moment . . . quietly."

"Bad night?" she said, walking in and settling into a chair opposite his desk.

"Never debate with yourself," he replied, touching his forehead.

"You're right," she said. "Because one of you will always lose."

"I'm afraid that both of us lost last night," he replied, touching his forehead again. "Sorry, but I guess I'm having serious worries about the implications of what we're—what I'm doing. And yet . . . damn it!" He stopped and pointed to Landsman's diary lying on the desk. "At least our salvage operation yesterday was a success. And I found a second will last night—or a copy of one, at least—as well as his most recent datebooks. The only trouble is that the will is incomplete, and I have no idea if it was ever filed or signed."

"And what about the datebooks? Are they helpful? Any clues about what he was intending?"

"So far as I can tell, just his life set down in abbreviations. I thought at first it might be some sort of code, but then I realized, who would bother with that in a document no one else would ever read? Anyway, I think I've figured out a few easy entries: AP for *appointment*, DN for *dinner*, and lots of names."

"That seems logical enough."

"So, Sally, why don't you take this most recent diary back to your desk and see what you can discover that might be relevant? Look for an appointment with someone at the firm or the names of any of the partners— that's obvious. But anything else that might indicate why he was thinking of revising his will and if he really did go through with it. It's doubtful that he'd detail his ruminations in a datebook, but who knows? But there might be something. And maybe some details about the new beneficiaries."

Sally took the book that he handed to her.

"I'm sorry to push this onto you," he continued, thinking he saw a look of disappointment on her face. "But I think you might be sharper at spotting something than I am, certainly this morning."

"Well," she said, standing up. "I'm never one to question a compliment. That's rare enough here on the bottom floor—to coin a term—among an 'eloquence' or maybe, in this case, I should say a 'disputation' of junior lawyers clawing at each other for a rung on the ladder."

"You're a great help, Sally," he said as he watched her leave the office. It was reassuring that he was alert enough to note the dark-blue ensemble she was wearing, a costume that advertised serious intent, yet there was that silhouette of hers that hinted at something else and a lot more intriguing.

After a moment, he turned on his computer, signed in, and read a few email messages, leaving most of them unanswered. His physical misery was beginning to dissipate, now diluted by several cups of the sour coffee he had brewed in the associates' basement lounge. Then, suddenly, quite unexpectedly, he thought, *I've been visited by the wrong nightmare! It's not my doubts that were disputing my sleep, but now that I think about it, I'm sure I was trying to figure out how to find the person who ordered the storage of Landsman's possessions and the destruction of his documents.*

He picked up the phone with one hand and thumbed through his address book for the number of the disposal company he had written down with the other.

A woman answered the phone almost as soon as he punched in the number.

Adam didn't hesitate: "This is Adam Chauncey speaking. I have a contract with your company regarding the possessions of a Mr. Percy Landsman, deceased."

"Yes, Mr. Chauncey. Is there some problem?"

"Indeed there is. I need to know who ordered the immediate removal of Mr. Landsman's apartment and the storage of his possessions."

The woman hesitated, cleared her throat, and finally said, "Why, you did, Mr. Chauncey. I spoke to you just . . . Let me see . . . It was two days ago in the evening. Yes, I'm sure I remember because it was a bit unusual. You asked to move up the date of our contract, which I did right then. Is something the matter? Did the trucking company fail to pick up everything? I didn't go to the apartment to check things out yet. We always do a follow-up just to make sure that the premises are tidy, but I haven't gotten around to it yet."

"Are you sure it was me?"

"Oh, Mr. Chauncey, you're teasing me. Of course, it was you."

"If you say so. And thank you, Miss . . . ?"

"Rogers, Roberta Rogers."

"Then it must be so, Miss Rogers."

"My, my," she said. "It certainly was."

Adam put the phone down carefully. "But it wasn't," he said. "Fuck! And the most I've just accomplished is making a fool out of myself with someone who thinks I was flirting with her or suffering from severe dementia."

He sat for a moment, trying to imagine who might have been responsible for this mix-up, if that's what it was. And then he stood up abruptly and hurried out of his office and into the large room where the paralegals worked. There was little noise except for the hum of the overhead vents: too cool in summer, stifling in winter, and always a mismatch during Chicago's fickle fall and spring.

A young man sitting next to the door looked away from his computer and eyed him curiously when he entered. It certainly wasn't so much a breach of etiquette for a junior associate to personally enter this space as it was a denial of the protocols of hierarchy in the firm. Sally's desk stood in the far corner, and she turned to face the door when she sensed the slight commotion as he entered. Almost immediately, she stood and walked over to join him.

"You didn't have to come to get me," she said.

"I know," he replied as they walked into the hallway. "I just couldn't sit still. Come into my office, and I'll tell you why. And if that's Landsman's diary and the notes on your desk, bring them along too."

When they were both seated at his conference table, he began, "I don't know what's going on, Sally, but I think someone . . . Let me start again. I'm sure someone in the firm is trying to sabotage our efforts to find out if Landsman's new will is legitimate."

"What do you mean?"

"I just called the disposal company, and they claim that I ordered the immediate storage of his possessions and the destruction of his papers."

"But of course you didn't. But who?"

"Doesn't matter right now to know that, although I certainly have my suspicions. But anyone could have said it was me. Except that it means two things: someone is watching us and that someone certainly doesn't want the original will to be contested."

"So what are you going to do?"

"Maybe change my mind, to begin with. What do you think?"

"Meaning?"

"I had been seriously thinking of ending our search right away. Get on with probate and stop trying to second-guess the intentions of a dead man I never met—and don't think I'd like very much."

"But that's not really serious, is it?"

"And now I'm convinced there's something strange going on here at the firm. Maybe something illegal or at least underhanded. Why else?"

He stopped and looked at her, trying to read the odd expression that suddenly spread across her face.

"Do you want my opinion?" she asked.

"Of course I do."

"Then here it is. I'll begin with the consequences. If you . . . if we continue to investigate, it might well be the end for both of us at the firm. Are you willing to run that risk?"

He didn't hesitate: "Well, I certainly don't want to. And my only hesitation is what happens to you. But I'm afraid it's too late—even for regrets. I'm pretty sure now that this was a kind of setup from the beginning. Putting me as co-executor. Someone with no experience, just a junior flunky who would follow the rules to the letter and never ask a question. Maybe that part was innocent or not, and we'll probably never know. But then there was my conference with Emsback the moment the higher-ups sniffed trouble and Bill Evans's too-convenient loss of memory. Too many things, Sally."

"You sound convinced."

"Becoming so. And I really wonder if my niche here in the basement of Smithson and Dwyer was ever all that secure anyway. Who knows if I'd ever make partner with all the competition? It never made sense that I got this position in the first place. My questionable background and a law degree from nowhere important. And is it not that very uncertainty that keeps us sitting late hours at our desks and jostling for attention from the partners and living like an urban hermit? A life of empty pizza boxes, stale beer, and solitary, anxious nights. Just waiting for that day when we ride the elevator upstairs for the last time and trade our cinder block offices for oak paneling. That's when life can begin all over again, if it ever comes. And now—"

"You sound really bitter, Adam."

"I'm not at all! That's the irony. It's what I wanted. At least I used to think I did. And sure, it's what any junior associate would desire. We'll put up with anything just to get on with it. But right now, I'm mostly distressed that I've brought you into this and put your job on the line too."

"Isn't there an outside chance it's just a mistake? Maybe there's some simple explanation, just a series of coincidences."

"You don't really think that, do you, Sally?"

She paused, and the worry lines on her face relaxed. "No. If I'm honest, I don't."

"That's what I want from you, Sally—honesty."

"That may be more than you bargained for."

"I'll chance it," he said.

"So now, what do we do?"

"That depends on what you've found in his diaries."

"Well, to begin with," Sally said as she pushed the small book to the middle of the table and then placed a manila file next to it, "you were right about how he recorded everything—abbreviations mainly, telephone numbers, a few words here and there. And about two months ago, the name Lopez appears, and then Sanchez for the first time a bit later. And Lopez has a circle around it. But it's Sanchez that we're looking for, right? Anyway, the name is spelled out just once, but I think later references are simply recorded as SN. There are three altogether. And nothing more about Lopez that I can find."

"It's got to be Sanchez-Lopez—the same name on the new will. It's the same person. The way you sometimes put Spanish names together when you marry." He paused: "Did you find any phone numbers or addresses?"

"Nothing. Of course, that might have been on his cell phone."

"And that's missing. And I would guess it's been destroyed. So we have to find this Sanchez person because not only is his or her name in the diary but also in those scribblings that look like Landsman was preparing his new bequests and then mentioned in the copy of the new will itself."

"I already did a cursory search online," Sally said, shaking her head. "And using the free white pages, which list only names with landlines, I found more than seventy-five Sanchezes in the immediate area. And how many cell phone users I wouldn't estimate, but it must be many, many more. Who has a landline these days anyway unless it's a business?"

"I'm not surprised," Adam said. "After all, this is Chicago. There must be thousands of people with the last name of Sanchez or Lopez, for that matter. Or even Sanchez-Lopez."

"Any other things in that diary that might help?"

"Well, yes, there's a couple of curious entries, again late last year: *Chpub* and *An.C*, both on the same date and the latter with an exclamation point."

"And do you have any idea what they might mean?"

"Yes. One is obvious: Chicago Public, although it could mean anything like a library, for example. But the *An.C* next to it is a mystery. And then, immediately following, there's a whole separate page of abbreviations, some of which are repeated elsewhere."

She pushed a sheet across the table for him to read.

He glanced at it and then exclaimed, "More abridgments! I don't understand Landsman at all. What a character! Why couldn't he just write things out like a normal person?"

Sally laughed. "So now you know what's normal? And you ask that working in a law firm?"

"OK, OK," he said, looking at the sheet of abbreviations, "but what in the world do *fil.pop, ad.S, an *, nnupt, Fa-Fa,* and *PY* mean? And this free-standing *L*? And, of course, *An.C.*"

"I'm as baffled as you are, but they have to be significant. Why else include them?"

Adam looked more carefully at the list. He picked up the paper and stared at it as if he could see through it to some hidden intention.

"Well, I'll be damned!" he blurted out. "I think two of these are Latin, maybe more."

"So you do remember your Latin?"

"Legal terms, of course. And there are a slew of them. But a few of these seem familiar to me. For example, look at this: 'Nnupt!' I think it has something to do with marriage. As for the rest, I don't know. It could be significant."

"So what do you plan to do?"

"Take this list to an expert."

"Here at the firm?"

"No. I'm betting that somewhere in the Chicago public schools, there's got to be someone who still teaches Latin. If we can't find anyone, maybe we could consult a Catholic priest. Would you mind calling around to see who might help us?"

"So, *art-pay uties-day?*"

"Huh? What? Oh," he looked at her smiling face and then he got it. "Touché! My god, pig Latin! It's been ages since I heard that. I guess that's a start. Yes, consider it *part of your duties. Ease-play.*"

She got up and left the room, pausing to look back at him for just a second, a curious smile on her face. But her expression was enough to make Adam wonder, did she resent all of this extra work that took her away from her duties? Was she concerned about her job at the firm? Or was there the hint of a personal message that she was conveying? He returned to his desk and looked at his schedule for the day. Nothing much planned except to plow into a pile of work that had been drifting into his file like a surprise Chicago spring snowstorm.

Toward noon, Sally returned, knocking first at his door and then entering without waiting for him to respond. "I've found several schools around the city that offer Latin," she said. "Mostly private academies—just what I expected. Chicago Latin is the closest. It's in Old Town. I made an appointment to see a Miss Haskins there at three. If that's not convenient, I can change it, but I thought you'd want to go today."

"Nothing on the docket so far, so if you don't mind being chauffeur, we could leave here about two-thirty."

"At your *'ommand-cay.*'"

"OK. Stop it! You'll regret that you started with pig Latin. How about lunch? I think I owe you."

"You certainly do, big time," she said. "Except I can't today. I've already got plans. But I'll hold you to it. You're running up quite a tab."

"I know, but what's the point if you won't let me pay it off?"

She said nothing, turned, and walked quickly out of the room, leaving him with an uneasy feeling that the only link between them was his prerogative to ask for her help. He knew he could either fret about it, turning over every conversation they had, looking for signs that she was interested, or just forget it. But that was just like him, he knew, to pay attention to the minutiae of their interactions, looking for some optimistic tone, some hint to hang his hopes on. It was part of his soul—at least the part he had inherited from his mother—to imagine all the best outcomes. But the only other choice was simply to get to work on executing a legitimate will that was already taking up far too much of his time. Do what was expected of him, except that he couldn't.

They arrived at the campus of Chicago Latin just before 3:00 p.m., Sally driving again. They hadn't said much on the way up north from the Loop because the early rush was beginning to accumulate with its stop and start traffic and the odd rude speedster. He could see that Sally was concentrating, and on occasion, he cursed a driver who cut them off.

"You tell 'em, Adam," she said after one particularly egregious instance that made her jam on the brakes and swerve onto the shoulder. But he didn't ask what had been festering all afternoon: what he should have said to her much earlier before the shelf life of his question had expired. He wanted to know who her lunch partner had been—"her plans"—but it was too late to ask now. It would suggest that he was somehow worried or too interested, prying—which was the truth, of course.

Sally pulled into the near parking lot, ignoring the warning that it was available only for faculty. When Adam started to protest, Sally just said, "We're here to see faculty, aren't we? Shouldn't that count?"

He could only nod in agreement.

When they approached the main entrance, Chicago Latin seemed to be a building of borrowed idioms and second thoughts. It had the odd, geometric shape of the New Brutalism, with an abrupt third-story overhang that jutted out a good ten feet from the rest of the structure. The windows were long and narrow, Prairie style, and one end of the building was hoisted on pillars as if the whole structure might someday decide to walk away and relocate somewhere else if the neighborhood declined. What saved it from the rough concrete desolation of its architectural cohorts, however, was the warm color of the brown brick cladding, which gave the whole school an inviting, friendly appearance. It was as if the architects had changed their minds several times and decided finally that the teaching of humanistic values inside ought to be reflected on the exterior of the building.

Passing through the metal detector at the entrance, they approached the monitor's desk located in a foyer that opened into three hallways. Adam didn't need to say anything; he was sure that Sally was as dismayed as he was at this state-of-the-art security guarding the school.

"May I help you?" asked the woman sitting behind the desk, glancing up at them. He was sure that they had interrupted some cell phone conversation or maybe a Google search. But then, moving closer, he saw that she had been reading a book. It surprised him, but perhaps she was a teacher on duty at the reception. He thought he should stop jumping to conclusions.

"We have an appointment with a Miss Haskins, the Latin teacher," he said.

The woman closed her book and shuffled some papers around. "Yes, here it is. I have a note from her. Mr. Chauncey. You're to go to her classroom, just down the hall to your left, about halfway. Room 108. She said to send you along as soon as you arrived." She glanced at a tiny wristwatch on her right arm. "You can go now. She's expecting you."

"Thank you," Sally said.

They walked into the brightly lighted corridor. There were trophy cases on one side—not for athletics but pictures of students who had won academic contests like Odyssey of the Mind and the Academic Decathlon—contests that Adam's comprehensive high school in Southern Illinois had probably never even heard of.

They stopped in front of the door to Room 108. A dim light shone through the opaque glass in the upper half.

Adam knocked gently. Hearing nothing, he pushed the door open, and they stepped inside.

It was a small classroom with neat rows of desks and chairs, recessed overhead lights, and narrow streamers of bright sunshine coming through the windows. All around the walls, there were pictures of ancient Rome: the broken splendor of the Colosseum, photographs of statues with their noses chiseled off, the lonely ruins of the Forum, and one majestic photograph of a volcanic mountain. Vesuvius? Adam wondered. And on a plaque over the door was the motto: "De omnibus dubitandum."

Sitting at a table beneath the blackboard was a tiny woman. She stood up as they approached and said, "You must be the lawyers from Downtown."

She waved her hand, indicating the front row of desks, and Adam and Sally sat down.

"It seems a very long time since I've been in a Latin classroom, Miss Haskins," Adam said.

"You must be Mr. Chauncey. And Miss . . . ?"

"Warren."

"How can I help you?"

"Yes, and thank you very much for seeing us on such short notice," he continued. "It has to do with a legal case we're investigating. Something we think might concern Latin or Latin abbreviations. My assistant will show you."

Sally stood up and handed the teacher the sheet of paper she pulled from a file she was carrying.

"It's not often that a Latin teacher is called on for expert advice or to testify in court, for that matter," Miss Haskins said as she took the paper and sat back down at the table. She took a pair of rimless glasses from her breast pocket and settled them on the bridge of her nose.

As she studied the paper, Adam looked carefully at her. She had to be in her late fifties or early sixties with gray hair roped in a braid across the top of her head. She was wearing a dark-red suit that suddenly reminded him of his mother, and he wondered just for a moment what it must have been like years ago to be in her class.

Miss Haskins's face looked almost fierce with frozen furrows as she studied the paper, although her lips moved slightly, perhaps as she pronounced the letters. And then a cautious smile smoothed the lines of her face. Quite unexpectedly, she laughed out loud.

"Yes, indeed, some of these entries are in Latin: at least two I'm familiar with. But I can even tell you more."

"That's wonderful," Adam said.

"The first one here, *Fil pop*, is *filius populii*."

"Meaning?"

"Male child born out of wedlock. A bastard," she said with surprising emphasis.

Sally tried not to look shocked.

"And this one *Nnupt* is *non nupti*, except it's undoubtedly a bad translation. It should be *non accepit*. But in any case, it must indicate 'not married.'"

She paused, clearly enjoying the puzzled looks on their faces.

"But these two and all the rest have another meaning. I'm surprised you didn't figure it out."

"But you'll tell us," Adam said.

"Indeed I will. I think that all of these others are genealogical abbreviations. Whatever their purpose here, they are notations that are widely used in ancestor research—a kind of shorthand. I'm sure if you go on the Web or even consult a genealogist, you can decipher all of them. But most aren't complicated. I'd guess that *Ad.S* means 'adopted son,' for example."

"That's amazing," Sally said. "You're such a great help."

"Not at all," Miss Haskins replied. "I only know because I've done some genealogical research myself. And once you get into it, you see all sorts of abbreviations like this. There's only one that I don't understand. Perhaps it's a mistake, but I can't place it. It's strange. *Fa-Fa*, literally meaning 'father-father,' which makes no sense. But for all the rest, the meanings are quite clear."

"Thank you so much for your help," Adam said, standing up. "It's a wonderful classroom you have, the pictures and all. You must enjoy teaching about ancient Rome."

"I do love it," she replied enthusiastically. "I only wish that my students shared your opinion. It's not a dead language, you see, or even a dead civilization," she continued, "but civilization itself! We have so much to learn from them. They're an unseen presence in the way that the past is always everywhere around us. If only my youngsters would recognize that."

Sally retrieved the paper, and she and Adam walked to the door.

"There's just one thing, Miss Haskins. The motto over the door, I can't interpret it," Sally said.

"It means 'Suspect everything.' Just to remind my students how worldly the Romans were."

"Well," he said, "that seems to be very good advice these days. Thank you again, Miss Haskins."

"It's been a pleasure," she said and then hesitated. "Will I be asked to testify in court? Something like an expert witness? It would be the first time for me, but it might do so much for the study of Latin. The publicity would help immensely, you must realize."

"We'll let you know," Adam said, opening the door. "And thank you again."

"What a strange woman," Sally exclaimed once they were in the hallway and out of earshot. "So unexpected."

"Why do you say that?"

"Well, buried in the past like that and yet wanting to be part of the show."

"She's not the first woman I've met with contradictions," Adam said.

"And what exactly does that mean? Or shouldn't I ask?"

"Nothing more than what I said."

"Oh, then I understand. It's quite clear."

Sitting in the car on the way back, Adam watched the lights begin to blink on as they entered the deepening canyon of tall downtown buildings. The weak spring sun was lowering in the west, casting long gray dark shadows across the streets. It would be after 5:00 p.m. when they finally entered the offices, but he had decided to ask Sally to stay late so they could discuss the information that the Latin teacher had given them. He was about to speak when she said, "I've got an idea. Just came to me. Something that just struck me."

"Do you want to wait until we're inside?"

"No, I'm going to let you off. I'm busy early tonight."

"OK," Adam said, continuing to wonder about her mysterious life after hours—and if she was engaged in some sort of relationship.

"So I'll tell you what I'm thinking now. I'm convinced that the abbreviation *An.Com* is 'ancestors dot com.' I'm sure you know about it, the website that's always advertising about finding your heritage. It has to be, from everything we know now, that Percy Landsman was using it to search for his birth parents."

"Is it something reliable, do you think?"

"I suppose so since I think they do a DNA sample in addition to looking at all kinds of records."

"You've got to be right, Sally!"

"I think I am."

"OK. That gives me a night's work, then. I'll take everything home with me from the office and go through his papers once more. There's bound to be some notation if he found anything out."

"Unless, of course, the answer was eaten up by that shredding machine."

Adam hesitated and then remembered Miss Haskins's motto: "What was it? 'De omnibus dubitandum.' I'll always doubt," he said. "Yes, good advice tonight. Because I'm also going to try to discover who keeps throwing a monkey wrench into everything we're trying to find out."

"Maybe better to say, 'Running one step ahead of us and anticipating what we're doing,'" she laughed.

"Or just plain 'No one wants us to question that will.'"

Sally said nothing more as she drove into the deepening gloom of the Loop. She stopped in front of the office building, and Adam stepped out of the car.

"I'll take your file, OK? I want to try to write out the words to match the abbreviations."

"See you tomorrow then," she said and drove off, leaving him standing in front of the revolving door that opened into the building and the long, lonely night he anticipated. He remained outside for a moment, staring at her car until it became two red dots in the stream of traffic. He thought that there was something brusque about her departures, like a door slamming, something final and decisive. End of conversation when she said goodbye, leaving him with nothing left to say. It made him wonder about her. Of course, there might be no mystery at all. Perhaps she was simply a private person and uninterested in him outside of the paid hours of work. Yet when they were together, she was animated, quick-minded, and even flirtatious. Almost more of a puzzle than the Landsman will itself.

Reluctantly, he went back inside the building and took the corridor leading to the associates' offices. The utility lights had already switched on, and the corridor leading to his office was gloomy in the muted light. Halfway down the hallway, he passed by the night crew of cleaners dressed in blue work uniforms and chatting as they pulled their buckets and mops out of the storage closet. He started to greet them in Spanish but hesitated as he always did because he thought it might imply that anyone doing such a job would automatically speak that language. But that wasn't what made him rush on. It was his insecurity tonight, knowing that he was prejudicing his job (and Sally's) in pursuit of some whimsical truth. So he simply nodded to them and continued into his office.

He was certain that a few of the paralegals would still be working nearby, but it still felt lonely to be sitting at his desk after hours, as if it was a confession that he had nowhere better to be and no one to be with.

He switched on all the lights, even the desk lamp that he almost never used, and somehow this unnecessarily bright illumination cheered him up for the task that he faced. In fact, he realized that he was excited by what he and Sally had learned from the Latin teacher and anxious to go over the documents they had rescued from the Landsman estate.

His first task was easy. He opened his computer to a website that listed common abbreviations and quickly found that Miss Haskins was right. Several were associated with genealogy research and Landsman's search for his birth parents. Then he went back to the datebook that Sally had studied. And again, there was that singular entry that had stumped the Latin teacher: something very strange that seemed to be a mistake or confused handwriting: *Fa-Fa*. Yet Landsman's other abbreviations were all quite decipherable. From the list, he knew that *Fa* meant "father," but why a repetition? It made no sense. He stared at it and then pushed the diary aside to look through the other documents, hoping to find some response from *Ancestry.com* if, indeed, Landsman had consulted them.

Despite a very careful search, he found nothing. No doubt any correspondence, if it existed, had been eaten up by the shredding machine. Or maybe it had been on his (lost) computer. In any case, not to be found.

He looked at his watch. It was past 8:00 p.m., and even the most harried paralegals would have disappeared by now. And he realized that he was very hungry, or did he just need a drink? He wasn't sure, so he placed the files in a neat pile, closed his computer, and left the office no wiser than he had been a few hours before.

Only a few restaurants and bars were open in the Loop at this time of night except those around the theaters; most others catered to the busy lunch hours and happy hour, but now the streets seemed almost deserted. The gloom was even darker walking under the shadows of the Elevated, although it became suddenly noisy with the wince of steel on steel when a train roared overhead. Hopping into a cab, he decided to stop off at Briefs and Contracts on the way home. It wasn't his favorite place—too many lawyers or patrons pretending to be lawyers, but it had good food. Happy hour would have long passed into the dregs of the evening. Now there would be mainly serious drinkers or, like him, individuals with nowhere important to be.

Arriving at the front door, he paid off the cab and entered, standing for a moment before he headed to the bar. He ordered a scotch neat and then swiveled around to survey the room and the other patrons. There were several tables of mixed couples and a few empty booths toward the back. Like so many other restaurants and watering holes, this place was an acoustic muddle. The noise level was high as even the most muted conversations ricocheted off the smooth surfaces of the ceiling and tile flooring. Some kind of music was playing in the background; at least he could feel the thump of the bass, but the words of the song were blurred. A perfect atmosphere to bury yourself in the sounds of other people's revelries. He didn't care.

Then, looking down to the end of the bar, he spotted a lone woman with a tall glass of some colored drink with a paper umbrella in front of her. From this distance, he couldn't guess her age or much else about her except that her dress was dark—blue or black. When she turned to stare at him, he raised his glass in a half salute and then turned away to gaze at the mirrored wall behind the bar and the line-up of sparkling glasses and bottles.

A moment later, he realized that the woman had moved to the stool next to his. She placed her drink next to his.

"Lawyer?" she asked.

"Do I look that obvious?"

"Takes one to know one," she laughed. "We all have that lusting-to-be-a-partner look.'"

He could see that she was about his age, a glowing complexion despite the dim light of the bar, carefully made up, but still wearing a business suit.

"Smithson and Dwyer," he said.

"Meet Morgan and West," she replied, extending her hand.

"I don't know that firm," he said.

"Very small, new, aggressive. We have a small office downtown. Most of our business is corporate, but we do the odd divorce if the stakes are high enough. Nothing criminal."

"At least not officially," he said.

"You sound a bit cynical for a young man like you. I wouldn't have thought so for someone at Smithson. They have a pretty good reputation from where I stand."

"I suppose so—old men chasing old money. But nothing seems exactly the same when you're looking up from the basement."

"I can imagine it's fairly cutthroat."

"Well, all I can say is that they hire to fire. Only a few of us will ever squeeze through to a partnership."

"True everywhere, isn't it?"

"Yes, no doubt."

Both of them were silent for a moment, waiting for the other to shift away from the subject of law into something personal. But Adam was reluctant to start some sort of fruitless flirtation just to prove himself. And she just smiled.

"I'm Rebecca," she said finally.

"Adam Chauncey here." He raised his glass and touched it to hers.

If she expected some intimate question, he surprised her.

"Are you good at puzzles?" he asked.

She gave him a strange look and then said, "I can usually finish the *Times* crossword, if that's what you mean."

"I do. So here's a quiz for you. I've been looking at genealogy records and abbreviations, and I've come across something peculiar. Maybe you can guess what it means."

"I'll try."

"OK. The entry I found is *Fa-Fa. Fa* meaning 'father.' But it seems to me like a strange redundancy."

She paused for a moment and took a sip of her drink. "Oh, I think that's an easy one," she said. "You see the hyphen. That represents the word 'is.' So, therefore, 'The father is the father.'"

"That makes no sense."

"You'll have to figure out what it means. I agree that it's odd. But perhaps, if you weren't sure that you were legitimate, and you got a genetic screening of some sort or consulted some type of records, it would mean that you were . . . actually were legitimate, that is."

"That's amazing, Rebecca!" he replied, saluting her with his drink. "I think you might be right. And someone in doubt of their heritage— adopted, perhaps—discovers that his adopted father is actually his real father. That's crazy and unusual, but maybe that's what it means. Amazing! Thanks so much!"

"It's the wisdom of strangers."

"I have to buy you another drink, at least," he said, but just then, he heard the annoying ping of a message arriving on a cell phone.

"I'd love to," she replied, digging into a purse that she pulled up from the floor, "but this is a reminder. I have to leave now. Just stopped in for a moment. I'm meeting someone."

"Well, Ms. Rebecca from Morgan and West, I can't thank you enough. You've earned your retainer tonight!"

"If only the law was so simple. Good night, Adam from Smithson and Dwyer, and good luck," she said as she slid off the stool and walked over to pick her coat off the track near the entrance to the bar. But suddenly she stopped, turned around, and came back. She handed him a card that she had retrieved from her purse. "Just in case you ever need a good lawyer," she said.

He glanced at it, put it in his vest pocket, and then watched as she disappeared out the front door. As soon as she was gone, he paid for his drink, called for an Uber, and paced around outside on the sidewalk until it finally appeared.

Sitting on the couch in his apartment, fighting off the hunger he felt, Adam picked up the phone and then set it back down again abruptly. He was too excited to eat anything, and he knew if he went foraging in the kitchen, his search would turn up nothing more than a few stale cookies, an orange or two, and coffee. Not a menu to calm his jitters. He wanted to call Sally with his speculation about Landsman's father and share with her the puzzle of the adoption. But he was reluctant. Not that it was too late, but he didn't want to discover that she wasn't home tonight.

And no doubt, he feared what he would find out if he learned more about her. Maybe she was just secretive, or maybe he was just getting her wrong. Maybe the explanation was entirely simple: her friendliness during office hours was exactly that. Beyond that, she wanted nothing more from him. Or maybe he just didn't understand her.

So instead of calling, he opened a bottle of wine, took it and a glass, and went into his study to think about what he had learned or thought he had discovered in his brief conversation at the bar.

Placing a fresh sheet of paper in the center of the bright pool of light from his desk lamp, he picked up a pencil and sketched a bare family tree, beginning with an empty T. On either side of the top cross, he wrote the names of Landsman's mother and father and below the father's name, the name Percy Landsman (adopted). He added a second stem and the name Eric Landsman (legitimate). And then, extending out from Percy's name, he scribbled a broken line to some unknown woman—his mother. And then he opened up the file of his notes and looked for the names that Sally had found: Lopez and Sanchez. He was pretty certain that Lopez must be his mother and that she had married someone named Sanchez. He wrote both names at the end of the broken line and then extended another line down to Percy from his father's name and a loop over to the identity of the mother. But why would he adopt his own son, even if this unknown women was his mother? It made no sense. Maybe Sally could figure it out tomorrow.

He turned off the light and went to bed, hoping that the alcohol he had consumed would lull him to sleep. But he only dozed fitfully, waking up once so restless that he got up, drank a glass of water, and then sat by the window, staring out into the darkness. He could hear an occasional car pass by the front of the building, but there was no noise in the alley. None of the apartments across the way were lighted, but a single street lamp reflected off several parked cars. He could make out a small deck on one of the buildings to his left. Turning to his right, he thought he could see the leaves of some flowers hanging from a window box. They looked black in the gloom.

Finally, he was able to sleep, but almost immediately, it seemed, the alarm on his clock radio chirped. He lay still for a minute, exhausted and not quite sure where he was. And then a wave of recognition washed over him: he wasn't on vacation at a resort somewhere with palm trees and a huge flat beach and rolling waves. He wasn't back in Southern Illinois, hearing his mother call him to breakfast. He was in Chicago, just a junior lawyer in a distinguished law firm, and about to be reprimanded or worse for breaking all the rules in the game of advancement. What the hell, he thought as he sat up.

He dressed with extra care this morning as if a neat appearance would conceal his disheveled mood. Entering his office, he turned on the computer only to find a message that looked both urgent and ominous. "Please make an appointment to see me at your convenience," it said and was signed by Frank Emsback. He knew he had to go immediately. For an associate like him, there was no 'convenience.' It meant right now, and the shorter the message, the more insistent.

He dialed the number of Ted Smith, the receptionist who made the partners' appointments and found that Mr. Emsback was in a conference but would see him at 10:30 a.m. Even though he had only exchanged a few words with Smith, Adam was sure that he detected some inflection of satisfaction in the other man's voice, as if the smile or perhaps the smirk on his face could somehow be transmitted through sound.

There was still time to brief Sally about his speculations, and he called her as soon as he hung up.

She appeared a moment later, pausing at the door as she always did and looking brilliant and fresh . . . as she always did.

"Come in, Sally, and sit down. I have something to show you."

When they were both seated at his conference table, he shoved his previous night's jottings across to her.

"What's this?" she asked. "It looks like Sudoku with names."

"Just look at it and tell me what you think."

She studied the paper for a moment and then looked up at him.

"This is the Landsman family tree."

"Yes."

"But I don't quite understand it. You've indicated that Percy was actually his adopted father's son with some unknown woman named Lopez as the mother."

"Yes. I think it might work that way."

Sally was quiet for a moment, and then she looked at him and laughed. "This is crazy, but I can think of only one reason why you might be right." She waited for a reaction, but Adam just stared at the paper. "Here's the only plausible way to make sense of this . . . if, of course, you're right. If Percy's father is, in fact, Mr. Landsman, the man who adopted him, it can mean only one thing."

"Don't keep me in suspense, Sally!"

"OK. Then here's what I think: Mr. Landsman has a child out of wedlock with a woman either named Lopez or Sanchez. Remember, from what Percy's brother told us, he had an affair with a housekeeper, wasn't it? So it must be her. And to protect himself, the father's name was withheld on the birth certificate. And then he adopts the child as his own son. The housekeeper is fired or leaves, and they invent the story that she died in childbirth."

"You're a genius, Sally! That has to be it! It's just crazy enough to be true. And from the jottings in his diary, it seems that Percy Landsman had figured it out also."

"All I can think of is the hurt he must have felt when he discovered it."

"What do you mean?"

"Imagine that you find out you lived your whole life with a man who was ashamed to admit he was your father! All those years of wondering who you really were, and the answer was sitting across the dining room table, telling you which fork to use."

"But he was adopted. Doesn't that count for something?"

"I have no idea what was going through the mind of the elder Landsman when he made that decision, but do you really think adoption is great for a child? Wouldn't you always think you were second best—a rejected child by your real parents? Some sort of unfortunate accident? Doesn't matter what the reason is. There has to be some strong feeling that you weren't wanted, cast aside and then picked up in some consignment shop. I think it's a terrible thing to do to a child. And there's Percy finding it out just before he died and then trying to find his birth mother, wanting to know if he had another family and if she had lived. It must have been awful or strange. And all the lies!"

"I understand what you're saying, Sally. I have to stop thinking like a lawyer for once and consider how I'd react."

"Didn't you tell me that your own father died when you were very young? What was that like?"

"Jealousy," Adam said.

"Meaning?"

"All my friends had fathers, and when I was a kid, even into high school, I used to think how great it would be to have someone cheering me on from the sidelines or even punishing me for my stupidities. When I was very little, I used to pretend that he was somewhere off in the army or an explorer or on some other secret adventure and that he'd return almost any day. And sometimes, if a man spoke to my mother after church or in a store or said hello on the street, I'd ask her if that was my father. Because she could never bring herself to tell me he had died—that is, until later. Of course, she meant well. She was sweet and kind, but to her, everything that happened was for the best. Except how could that be? You know you can only stand so much optimism until it eventually curdles into something dark and treacly. What I mean to say about Percy is that I think I can sympathize with the empty feeling of being adopted, of missing a crucial link in your identity."

Sally just looked at him for a moment, and he thought perhaps he had said too much—revealed a part of him that she was embarrassed to see.

"I think that explains a lot," she said.

"Meaning?"

"Why you're so invested in this, just like Percy was."

"Maybe. Or maybe it's just my love of a puzzle."

There was an uncomfortable silence between them for the next minute or so as if they had approached that awkward point of intimacy.

"So do you think that Landsman actually located his birth mother and maybe her family if she married, and that's why he was trying to change his will?" she finally said.

"I think that's it, exactly. And my bet is that the woman's name was either Lopez or Sanchez. Must be the former. And then she married someone named Sanchez and became Sanchez-Lopez."

"Of course. That has to be it. So now we have to find her ourselves. I know there wasn't any address in his diary that wasn't linked to a doctor or some financial institution. I checked carefully."

"And finding the right Sanchez. My god! Even if she remained in Chicago!"

"There is a way," he said. "But we'll need to find the record of Percy's adoption and the birth certificate if it's written somewhere in the papers we have. We'll have to go through everything again, knowing what we're looking for now. I'm betting the birth certificate says 'father unknown.' I remember Eric Landsman saying that the mother died in childbirth. But that's surely a lie. Who knows? And it certainly doesn't matter at this point."

"Can we apply for the records ourselves?"

"No. I'm sure not without a court order. Birth and adoption records are sealed unless, for some reason, the person has made them public. And in this case—" Just as he was about to continue, his desk phone sounded, and he instinctively looked at his watch. He jumped up from the table and seized the receiver. "Yes," he said. "I'm on my way." As he rushed out the door, he said, "Summons from on high." What he actually thought was more like "Judgment Day."

Emerging from the elevator into the lobby of the partners' wing, he brushed past the reception desk without stopping to ask for permission and walked quickly down the corridor to Frank Emsback's office. Passing by the secretary without a glance at her, he found that the inner door was ajar, and he pushed it open without knocking. He started to apologize for being late but stopped abruptly. Sitting at the conference table were two partners: Emsback and John Dwyer himself. Almost without thinking about it, he straightened his tie, buttoned his suit coat, and stepped into the room.

"Come in, young man," Emsback said, half standing from his chair. "You know John Dwyer, of course. Sit down." The gesture he made with his hand was like a friendly invitation withdrawn.

Adam thought he should shake hands with both men, but neither of them made the slightest offer, so he pulled a chair away from the table and sat down.

"Yes, how are you, sir? I'm sorry to be late," he said.

"Never mind," said Dwyer with a brief smile that cut across his face. "We're not on billable hours."

Adam had the clear impression that this slim effort at a joke was designed to put him at ease. Disarm him? But it didn't, and the silence that followed just made him more nervous.

"Are you happy here?" Dwyer asked finally.

"Yes, sir," Adam replied. "Very. I love my work."

"Good boy," Dwyer continued. "I remember my first days—weren't always easy. You may think that because my father founded the firm, I just could just sail in through the door and make partner. But he was a crusty old cuss, and he drove me harder than anyone just to prove a point. Made my life a misery of long nights and all my days measured out on yellow legal pads. We didn't have paralegals in those days, so I had to do all my own research. My old man was the sort you couldn't imagine that ever had a childhood—at least I never saw him that way. I think he was born with a tie and suspenders." He stopped, smiled a steely smile, and looked intently at Adam. "We're treating you OK, then, are we?"

"Yes, sir," Adam said, glancing at Emsback, who was watching silently, "I have no complaints about the work. None at all."

"Good then. Because we have a special project we'd like you to work on. It'll take all of your time from now on. Emsback here will fill you in on the details. He'll be your lead."

"And this project?"

"One of the big department stores here in the Loop is looking to sell out, actually part of a consolidation. Business isn't what it used to be, you know. Carriage trade is mostly gone online these days. You can tell just by walking outside and looking at who's on the sidewalk and, more important, who isn't there. I don't think my wife has come downtown to shop in a year. Not like after the war or even the fifties. But anyway, center cities are closing up shops everywhere, even here in Chicago. So they're selling out. And I'd like to have you work on the contracts. It'll be complicated and demanding. What do you think?"

"I'd be happy to work on it, of course."

"Are you doing something else now?" Dwyer asked.

"Just finishing up with a will probate. I'm the executor. And a few other minor things."

"Get done with it then. This'll take up all your time and then some."

"Yes, sir," Adam said, "it sounds like a great opportunity."

Emsback spoke finally, "I'll be sending you some preliminary work we've done, and we'll need to schedule several meetings with the owners and then with the lawyers of the purchasers. So clear your calendar, Chauncey. And finish that damned will."

"All right," Adam said, pushing back his chair. "If there isn't anything else, I'll get right on it."

"Good boy," Dwyer said, "I'm putting my trust in you."

Adam stood up, nodded slightly, and went out of the room, closing the door carefully behind him. As he passed through the main lobby, the receptionist smiled at him as if the two of them shared a secret. But instead of taking the elevator, he turned down the other corridor toward the secretaries' workspace. He spotted Lizbeth Lowry in the corner, at her desk, and motioned to her.

"I'm beginning to suspect you only visit me when you want something," she said when she joined him in the hall.

"Do you have time for a coffee?" he asked.

"Not even a decaf," she replied. "So what brings you up to the Tower?"

"I'll bet you know more than I do, Lizzy," he said. "Something about an assignment to work on a big department store sale, except that I think it's only a pretext."

"For what?"

"To stop me investigating the Landsman will. Am I right?"

She gave him a long, serious look and finally said, "I have to get back to work now."

"But . . ."

"I can only tell you to be careful, Adam. Watch what you're doing."

"Because they're watching me? Is that it?"

"Nice to see you again, Adam," she said, turning back toward the door. "Do come up and see me sometime when you're not so busy. And make it a social call next time."

He stood for a minute, watching her make her way back to her desk and then walked to the elevator.

It was a relief to be back down on the associates' floor and in his own office. He called Sally immediately.

When she appeared at the door, he said, "Come in, come in!"

"Was it bad? You look very strange."

"The big guns were out," he said. "They must be very worried because Mr. Dwyer himself wanted to see me. Put me on a team working on the contract for the sale of a department store. But didn't tell me which one. Here in the Loop, however. And Emsback was there, silent as a ghost until the very end when he told me in no uncertain terms to get done with the will."

"They're really worried, aren't they?"

"Yes, and worse, because when a partner starts telling you about his personal life, watch out!"

"Dwyer did that?"

"Yes, some story about how tough his father was and the bad old days of Chicago."

"That is serious."

"You got it, and I stopped by to ask Lizbeth Lowry what was going on, but she was mum as a statue."

"So what about the new will? Are you going to drop it?"

"That's what they want, but I don't see how I can. And there's one thing I have to know immediately. I need to look at Landsman Senior's will. It's a really long shot, and I doubt we'll learn anything. But I want you to contact the Circuit Court Archives and order a copy. Maybe it's our only chance of finding Lopez or Sanchez and her heirs. That is if he left her some sort of legacy. And if the story of her death in childbirth is phony as we suspect."

"So, any bequests aside from young Percy and his brother."

"Yes, aside from his two sons."

For the next several days, Adam plunged into the minutiae of the department store contract, working upstairs most of the time and meeting several times with the attorneys representing the conglomerate that was absorbing the store and its various outlets around the city. It was complicated, boring work, and he went home every night, exhausted and empty after sparring with the pin-striped huddle of New York lawyers. In law school, it had been a standing debate after a couple of beers about what to call two lawyers gathered in a room. The possibilities had seemed endless. His very straight and unimaginative friends had looked it up on the Web and then argued for "an eloquence" or "an argument—those were the standard terms." Someone, a lot more cynical, had favored "a disgrace." But he thought a football metaphor described the profession best because it described coordinated aggression, the seizure of territory, and a complicated playbook. Yes, a "huddle" of lawyers.

Sitting in his office, mulling over the latest complicated paragraph in the merger, Adam was more than happy to hear a knock on the door. As he had hoped, it was Sally.

She breezed into the office, clutching a file, which she laid down on his desk.

"Here it is. The elder Landsman will. Full of surprises."

"Sit down," he said as he began to glance through it. Coming to the section on bequests, he found a long list of charities, with most of his estate divided between his surviving wife and equal shares to his two sons, Eric and Percy. There was, however, one small gift to a Maria Lopez.

"This is amazing! You were right, Sally. That confirms what Eric Landsman told us: his father had an affair with some sort of household servant. This has to be her, except that she didn't die in childbirth. And, of course, there's an address. Dated, of course. Damn! After all this, we're going to find out what Percy must have discovered."

"So now what?" she asked. "You're up to your ears in contract negotiations."

"I know, Sally, and eyes upstairs seem to be following me pretty closely. And I still haven't sent any will to probate, either. But what about you, Sally? Are you ready to do some more detective work? Track down this Maria Lopez or Sanchez-Lopez?"

"I suppose so, although no chance that she's still alive. It's been years. That must be a very old address."

"Yes, I know it's going to be really difficult, but I think you're up to it. Just one more problem before you put on your deerstalker hat."

"OK, Sherlock. And . . . ?"

"Sanchez. That second name. I'm sure Maria Lopez married and then changed her name."

"If you're right, we'll never find a trace of her."

"Probably not, but let's try. Two or three more days. I can't hold off probate much longer."

"OK," she said, standing and backing away from the desk. "I'll get onto it right now. But no promises."

"I don't expect any," he said, "but maybe a surprise."

Chapter 8

Sally drove southwest toward Humboldt Park. The address she was looking for, Maria Lopez's last known whereabouts, was a discouraging-looking apartment building of about four stories, the sort of structure that you'd never notice because of its ubiquity—a residence, she thought, of no particular design, constructed of indifferent yellow brick, with two square wings and a recessed entrance. The large first-floor windows were covered with a rusted iron grating. She walked up the sidewalk between the two rectangular sections of yard, brown with patches of winter burn, and then mounted the brick steps to the front door.

She hesitated for a moment, thinking about this strange mission. There was no chance whatsoever that the current residents in the apartment would have any idea what had happened to Maria Lopez. Much too much time had passed—a whole generation. She blamed herself for giving in to Adam's whim, sending her on this fruitless chase after someone who had long since died. But when she thought about it, she wondered if this adventure was actually her fault, not his. Maybe she shouldn't have encouraged him to doubt the Landsman will in the first place. And she surely shouldn't think of this as an adventure! There was something unhealthy—no, just strange—about the way she and Adam acted together: like two daredevils standing before a deep precipice egging each other on. And now to appear at someone's door with a question they couldn't possibly answer. What was the purpose of that? But here she was, too late to listen to her any sensible thoughts.

She stood straight, shrugging her shoulders inside her coat and resolved to leave quickly once she confirmed that no one knew of Maria Lopez. She found the apartment number that the will had listed—301 on the call box—and dialed the code next to the name Narvaez. The phone rang several times, but there was no response, so she hung up and dialed again. Finally, a woman answered, speaking rapid Spanish.

Sally knew a few words but not enough to know if the voice was friendly or angry at being disturbed.

"This is Sally Warren," she said quickly in English. "I'm wondering if I might speak with you for a moment. I'm sorry to bother you, but this is very important."

There was a long silence, and Sally thought for a moment that the woman had hung up.

"All right. I buzz you in," she said. "But I'm not buyin' anything. Nada! Understood! So if you're sellin', take off!"

The door made a clunking sound as it unlocked, and Sally walked into a dreary lobby. There was no elevator, so she walked up the stairs to the third floor. Apartment 301 was open, and an elderly, frail-looking woman in a bathrobe was standing in the frame, her hand on the edge of the door as if she were ready to slam it shut in an instant.

"Thank you very much for seeing me," Sally said as she approached. "I won't take a minute of your time."

The woman made no gesture to let her into the apartment, and Sally could only see a corner of it from the half-open doorway.

She had to raise her voice above the sound of the TV set booming in the background. "I'm looking for someone who used to live in this apartment. Perhaps a very long time ago," she said. "Her name was Maria Lopez. Or maybe Sanchez-Lopez. It's important for me to find out about her."

The woman just stared at her and said nothing. She clutched her bathrobe tightly around her neck. Sally waited, thinking perhaps she hadn't heard. So she repeated the name even louder: "Maria Lopez."

"Heard you the first time," the woman said angrily. "Don't know why all you folks is coming 'round trying to find somebody used to live here. Just like I told that man before, I don't know no Maria Lopez or Sanchez. Never heard of her until now. What's goin' on with you people anyhow? Don't you talk to each other? Why are you bothering me?"

Sally tried to hold back her excitement, but she blurted out her next question: "Was it a man who came to see you? Did he tell you his name?"

"Didn't ask. Why should I? None of my business, is it?"

"Was he young or old?"

"White man, looked kinda feeble and real old. And that's all I know, and I'm not saying anything more. You people got to stop comin' round here, bothering me." She stepped back and slammed the door.

Sally stood for a minute, thinking about what the woman had told her. It was obviously Percy Landsman who had appeared there before her, tracing his birth mother. It had been the remotest chance that anyone knew Maria Lopez; way too much time had passed. But she had learned that they were on the right trail, walking right in the footprints left by Landsman. But where, she wondered, had he gone next? How had he found his family, as it seems he had? Yes, he must have, but where in the world were they?

Sitting back in her parked car, she dialed the law offices. When Adam answered, she began talking immediately: "I just finished talking to a woman who lives in the apartment that Maria Lopez or Sanchez-Lopez once occupied. No luck at all in tracing her, not that I expected it, but I did find out something really significant. She told me that someone had appeared only a few months ago, looking for Maria. I'm betting—in fact, I'm absolutely certain—it was Percy Landsman trying to track down his birth mother. But I'm at a dead end now. No leads at all. She couldn't tell me anything more."

"Pretty much what we expected, isn't it?" Adam asked. "Maybe you'd better come back to the office now. I'm afraid we'll never find out what Percy discovered. Thanks a lot, Sally. We had to pursue this to the last dim hope. But I think you're right—dead end."

Sally started the car, pulled away from the curb, and drove down the street. She would never have noticed or even looked around except that a truck at the next cross-section roared through a stop sign without stopping, and she had to slam on the brakes. She sat still for a moment, took a deep breath, and then looked around, very deliberately, to see if any other cars were approaching. And then she noticed a large structure to her right. It was a church with a large white statue of the Virgin Mary surrounded by low yew trees standing in front.

"Maybe, just maybe," she said under her breath and turned the corner, pulled up alongside, and parked. As she walked up the sidewalk, she noticed a small sign next to the entrance reading: "Nuestra Señora de los Siete Dolores." And incongruously embedded in the large cornerstone to the right of the large wooden front door was the number 1903 in what looked like lacey German script. Chicago! She said to herself, every newcomer leaves their mark!

She mounted three worn stone steps and tried pushing the door in, but it was firmly locked. To the right was a large cast-iron door knocker ring. She lifted it up and banged it against the metal plate mounted below it. She could hear the solid noise as it reverberated inside. She waited. As she was about to try again, she heard steps approaching and then the door swung in. A young man in black slacks and a black shirt with a white priest's collar stepped outside.

He looked at her with such a strange expression that she felt that she must immediately apologize. "I'm very sorry to intrude, Father. But I'm wondering if I might come in and talk to you for a moment. It's rather important."

He nodded and opened the door wider and stepped back.

In the dim light, she could see that the interior was very large and traditional, with a vaulted ceiling, rows of pews, and an elaborate chancel and crossing. Built, she thought, with another time and another culture in mind. The only objects that indicated anything about the contemporary parish were two large flags embracing the edges of the pulpit: one from Puerto Rico and the other, she guessed, from Mexico.

"How can I help you?" he asked.

She hoped he would ask her to sit down or maybe lead her to an office, but he remained standing, blocking the central aisle.

"I'm sorry," she said again. "And I know that this is just a very remote possibility, but I'm trying to find out the history of a woman named Maria Lopez or Sanchez, who might have been once a member of this parish many years ago. It's a matter of an inheritance. I represent a law firm from downtown. I know it's just an off chance, but I really had to stop in to see."

"Just a minute," he interrupted, looking at her intensely. "Come and sit down. This is very curious, very strange, indeed. The coincidence."

He indicated a pew on the left side of the aisle. He sat down opposite her.

For a moment, he just stared, his dark eyes squinting at her. Sally wondered if she should say something. She wanted to but managed to hold back her excitement.

"This is the second time that someone has come looking for Maria Lopez," he said and then paused as if he wondered if he should say anything more.

She just smiled at him and nodded.

"I wouldn't have remembered, but it seemed unusual. About three months ago, an elderly man—I have his name somewhere back in my office—came to see me and asked about Señora Lopez."

"Percy Landsman," she blurted out. "The name was Percy Landsman. I'm right, aren't I!"

"Perhaps something like that. It was a strange Anglo name. Yes, that sounds like it."

"What did he want? Could you tell him anything?" she asked.

"Please, Miss . . . ?"

"Sally Warren." She chided herself for interrupting. He was obviously very curious and probably enjoying himself as he related what seemed to be a very strange story.

"This man—yes, I think that name is right—wanted to find out if Maria Lopez had ever been a member of this church. We have lots of old records of marriages and baptisms. I thought it was a very strange request, and I knew it would take a very long time to look through records. And of course, there is no one alive now who would remember her. But I felt sorry for the man. He seemed ill and maybe a little desperate, and he explained that he was looking for traces of his mother. He said he had been adopted and that he had found the name of his mother and knew that she once lived down the street a very long time ago. But he couldn't find anything more about her. She just disappeared, and of course, he was sure that she died. But he wanted to know if there was still family in the area and if they had the same name or something different."

He paused, leaning back slightly, and continued, "It is true, given his own age, that his mother would have died many, many years before, but I thought if she married in the church, there might be a record. So I promised to look through all our old files. He even offered to pay me. But then, when I found something, he made a very large contribution to the church . . . for the roof."

"You found something?"

"Yes, finally, yes, I did. Maria Lopez married Enrique Sanchez here in this church. That is why she disappeared. She became someone else."

Sally could scarcely contain her excitement. "Do you know what happened to her then?"

The priest continued, "Well, yes, I found something more. Maria Sanchez-Lopez died a number of years ago. One of my predecessors officiated at the funeral."

"And that is all?"

"No," he said in a tone that told her not to stop him again. "There was a baptism. A boy. His name was, I think, Devante. Yes, Devante Sanchez. I remember it because one of my best friends at seminary was named Devante. It's an unusual name."

She said nothing but waited for more.

"Apparently, the Sanchez family remained in the neighborhood for a number of years and then finally moved away. *Desapareceda*. That's all I can tell you. Nothing more."

"And that's what you told Mr. Landsman?"

"Yes, except, now that I think of it, there was something more about Señor Sanchez in the records. He was very generous to the church. Not with money—I think the family was very poor. But he gave us time and talent. He was a mason, and this old building, as you can see, is needing many repairs all the time."

"Do you know where he went after here?" Sally asked.

"I have no idea."

"And did you see Mr. Landsman again?"

"Yes, but only the second time when I gave him the information."

"And that's all?"

"Well, only that we got a check from him later. I was embarrassed because it was so large. But, yes, that's all."

Sally stood up, held out her hand briefly, but then withdrew it. "That's amazing what you've told me, Father. Thank you so much."

He smiled at her with a look that said he was very pleased to help.

"It is nothing. The Church is a good parent and watches out for all its children."

"I can see that," she said.

Sitting in the car, she rummaged in her purse and picked out her cell phone. Dialing the number of Adam's office, she put the phone on the dash and started the engine. When he answered, she reached for it, but it slipped onto the floor. She could vaguely hear his voice, and she said loudly, "Just a minute. I dropped the phone."

When she had it firmly in her grip, she began without waiting: "There's wonderful news and then something you don't want to hear."

He said nothing, although she could picture the puzzled look on his face—the grimace he often made when he couldn't think of anything to say.

"Just by accident, I stopped into the Catholic Church near Maria Lopez's apartment, and the priest there said that Percy Landsman had visited a couple of months ago. It turns out that she was married in that church to a man named Sanchez, and they had a son. Baptized there. By the name of Devante."

"That's great, Sally. But what made you stop at the church?"

"Don't know, really, except that I saw it, and it struck me to ask."

"You're a genius! But is that all?"

"Yes. But that's also the bad news: there's nothing more. The family moved away years ago. The priest has no idea where they went. It could be anywhere. So, yet another dead end. It's so long ago. Who would remember, anyway?"

Adam was silent. "Come on back to the office," he said finally. "I was going to file the original will this afternoon. I don't see any reason to hold it up anymore. You're right. A very tantalizing dead end. Another one. But—"

"Are you sure?"

"I'm afraid so. The more we find out the further we seem to be from the truth. This has been a fool's errand from the very beginning. I don't know what I was thinking. Come on back. You're a marvel, Sally. But I'm afraid it's over. Whatever Percy Landsman discovered, he took to the grave."

"But there is that second incomplete will we found."

"Yes, I know, but it was only a preliminary sketch, a copy, and nothing legal."

"Adam, I don't understand. It's not like you to give up after all this."

"I don't know, Sally. I've been thinking while you were gone. It's just not worth it."

She started to speak but then stopped herself. No need to question his motivation if, as she suspected, he was thinking of the danger to his career. He was right. And she needed to stop encouraging him to risk it.

She hung up and sat for a few more minutes, turning a question over in her mind, again and again. What was it about finding your parents— your father and birth mother—that was so important? Percy Landsman first and vicariously, it seemed, even Adam Chauncey. Maybe it was just something she couldn't fathom because her own family had been so close. She had never wondered who she was and never doubted that she was just Sally Warner, an average daughter in an average family—two families, that is. Even when her mother had passed away three years ago and her father remarried a woman with two children, the memory of her remained a permanent bookmark in her own story. She would never have to question her identity. If she tried, perhaps she could understand the complicated feelings of not knowing a parent, never seeing them, never comparing yourself to them, not looking in the mirror of your birthright, not being able to observe the two adults to see yourself reflected in what they looked like, how they spoke, how they laughed, wondering what gestures and traits, what gifts or burdens were passed on to you. To have that only in halves or not at all, how much would that hurt? Maybe she had too much family to understand Adam or Percy Landsman.

But what was it with Adam, anyway? They were so close to discovering something, but now, suddenly he wanted to give up. She didn't want to think it, but she suspected that the interference from the Tower—the promises and threats—had finally sunk in and convinced him to give up. And maybe she had misjudged him from the beginning, thinking he was something more than a pushy junior clamoring to make partner.

She started the car and pulled away from the front of the church and drove back downtown. After she had parked in the lot underneath the adjacent building, she made her way back to Dwyer and Smithson and then to Adam's office.

"Sit down, Sally," he said when she entered through the open door. He stood up and closed it and made his way back to his desk. "I've had a chance to do some more thinking ever since you called. And, as I said on the phone, I'm convinced it's best to drop everything concerning Percy Landsman's family. I can't even remember now what made me so interested." Then he looked away from her as if he were talking to himself. "I need to get on with it and bury myself in the details of this merger contract I've been neglecting. It's pointless. Every time we've found something out about Landsman, all it ever did was lead us to another obstacle. It's time to be realistic and understand that there never was a puzzle—just something we—I mean, I invented. Maybe I've just been bored and looking for an adventure. But there aren't any adventures in corporate law—I know that. I've always known that. Just fucking dull billable routine, swimming through oceans of paper, trying to make partner . . . sometimes. Anyway," he continued, "you're a trooper. I appreciate everything, but I give up."

"That doesn't sound like you, Adam Chauncey, the person I know," she said. "Not for a minute. But I guess I couldn't imagine how to proceed from here anyway. So, I'll go back to the paralegal pen. I'm pretty certain that my desk is piled high with research requests." She stood up, looked intently at him, and then left without a further word.

Adam stared at the door she closed behind her as if he could see through it and observe her walking down the hallway. There was one awful thing about this moment. If he were honest with himself (and this seemed to be a day that called for honesty and self-examination), he had pursued the Landsman case half out of the pleasure of being with her. And now it was going to end. Maybe he'd try to ask her out in a few days, but maybe not, or maybe just for a coffee or lunch. He could never be sure of her attitude to him, her extracurricular feelings for him, if she even had any. Worse, she seemed so disappointed in him just now—not what she said exactly but the way her voice seemed tentative and her words unconvincing. It made him wonder why he was so bad at relationships— certainly nothing he could blame on his childhood. He didn't believe in the tenacity of past unhappiness for a minute. No, he would have to admit it; he just wasn't particularly good at anything but the law. And now he had to cease and desist with this case before it destroyed everything he ever thought he had wanted. Her most of all.

Chapter 9

Adam had never been particularly alert to catching moods or detecting changes in the office atmosphere. However, for the next week or so, whenever he passed a partner on a trip upstairs or, indeed, around the conference table, even his most mundane remark seemed to provoke everyone's momentary gaze as if he might be about to say something important. It seemed as if his presence was suddenly recognized but in an almost studied way. Of course, he knew the reason: the original will had been sent to probate, and he and Sally had returned to their familiar territories like eager beavers let loose to chew through a forest of legal documents, albeit now in separate streams.

If that observation should have reassured him, it only confirmed what he already knew—that this particular will had attracted unusual attention upstairs. Of course, the amount was tidy—a curious understatement if you thought about it. Could a large sum be sloppy, like a jumbled bag of dollar bills and loose coins? But that was just lawyer's slang for you: offhand and borrowed from who-knows-where. And there was nothing controversial or difficult about the will—the most straightforward of uncomplicated documents despite the mention of his birth family. It was only he and Sally who had questioned anything at all, and that was suggested by Landsman's curious diary and the tentative new will and its shifting list of bequests.

At times like this, he remembered what one of his professors had remarked during a particularly boring class on criminal law. It had been a late afternoon, and the elderly professor had been droning on, reminiscing about cases he had handled as district attorney of Rock Island County, Illinois. Adam hadn't been paying much attention, and the man's speech was muffled by age and indifference to his task. Moreover, the professor had the irritating habit of interjecting irrelevant explanations when he seemed to lose the thread of his argument—which was pretty often. In fact, only later did Adam remember the instructor's curious remark. "Every straight line has an angle." Of course, what he meant was clear enough—nothing in the law was obvious, and every argument had a potential flaw. He decided that it was a perfect motto for his profession, although maybe not something to hang on the wall for clients to see.

One particularly bright and optimistic Monday afternoon, following a weekend of no regrets and, for once, little homework, Sally knocked at his door. When she entered, he stirred slightly in his chair, thinking how fresh and lovely she looked, as if she had just emerged from a shower. In a moment, his imagination would begin to undress her, and he had to stop right there.

"Hi Sally," he said, standing up.

"I've been busy," she said and then paused. "I think I've found something about the Landsman will that you ought to know."

"And I was just thinking about how glad I was that it had been settled and all the loose ends tied up. And now—"

"I was sure you were thinking that," she continued, "but I just tried one last avenue to find any of his relations—the Maria Sanchez-Lopez family. I know you said we were through chasing this down, except I wanted to give it one last try. And I think I found something."

"I don't know, Sally. I'm really tired of chasing around Chicago, looking for ghosts. What's the point?"

"I thought you might say that, but I've found two names—the son's name. Only two Devante Sanchezes in the whole Chicago area. Maybe it's worth tracking them down, just to make sure."

"And what should we say when we find them? Knock on the door and announce that they won the lottery?"

She said nothing.

"Damn your persistence, Sally," he said. "I had a whole weekend of not thinking about Landsman or wills or anything. But I suppose we have to. How did you find them?"

"People Finder. It's a free service on the Web. I just typed in the name and general location. Of course, there's every chance in the world that the man we're looking for has moved away or is deceased."

"Look, I'm sorry. It's just that . . . But sure, you're right. It's worth trying, I agree. But just this once. Nothing more. So back on the trail of Percy Landsman for a last sortie. Let me finish up what I'm doing, and we can drive out this afternoon."

"Your chauffeur is ready anytime," she replied and walked out of the office.

Adam spent the next ten minutes plowing through a particularly boring and detailed contract element, almost unable to concentrate, recognizing that he was skipping words as he read and blurring whole sentences that he then had to revisit. He had to remind himself several times that he loved the law, except at times like this when he was preoccupied with minutiae. Several cups of bitter coffee that afternoon hadn't helped either and just made him jumpy rather than focused. This was surely not a time to be thinking about his future, but if that future meant being tethered to a desk, trying to translate obscurities into principles and ideas, well, maybe . . .

He didn't want to finish the thought.

It was after three when he finished writing up his commentary. Walking over to the paralegal section, he motioned to Sally, who grabbed her purse and joined him at the door.

"Ready?" he said.

"Yes."

"And you have the addresses?"

"Yes, the first is on Cullerton Street in the Pilsen area. I'll drive."

It took about half an hour to arrive in front of the small house wedged between two larger apartment buildings, like a younger sibling towered over by two grown-up brothers. It struck Adam as he looked at it now that the architecture of Chicago was a series of beginnings, an experimental incoherence that never rested. It was never monotonous but also never orderly.

Mounting the rickety wooden steps, he and Sally paused at the front door.

"This could just be a fool's errand," he said.

She just smiled at him and pushed the doorbell button. When no one answered, she knocked on the glass window.

After another minute, the curtain on the window moved slightly, and they could see someone peering out at them. Finally, the door opened enough to allow a yellow cat to squeeze through. An elderly woman, obscured by the shadows, looked out at them.

"Good afternoon," Adam said quickly. "I'm very sorry to bother you, but if you don't mind, we're looking for Devante Sanchez. Is he at home?"

The door opened wider, and they could see into the dimly lighted hallway where the woman stood. She was very short, wearing a pink bathrobe with matching pink slippers. Her black hair was streaked with strands of silver, and the back of her hands, gripping the doorframe, were wrinkled with prominent ropey blue veins.

She said nothing for a minute and then opened the door wider. "What do you want with him?" she asked.

"I'm a lawyer," Adam said, "and we're trying to find Devante Sanchez."

"You want to come in?"

"Yes, if we might?" Sally said.

The woman retreated, leaving the door open, and they entered behind her. She disappeared immediately around the corner into a small living room where a large television set rumbled in Spanish.

The woman sat down on a lumpy plush couch and looked at her guests and then back at the television screen.

"Sit please," she said, and Adam and Sally took the other two chairs in the room and sat opposite her.

For a moment, no one said anything, and then suddenly, the woman seized the television remote next to her and turned off the program.

"My novella," she said.

"We're sorry to interrupt," Sally said. "But could you tell us where to find Devante Sanchez?"

"No, I can't," the woman said. "I ain't seen him for years. He left."

"Are you Mrs. Sanchez?" Sally continued.

"Yes, I am . . . or was. Don't know what to call myself after so many years . . . *esposa . . . viuda.*" When she saw a puzzled look on their faces, she continued, "Widow. And I don't know where he is. Why're you looking?"

"Well," Adam said, "it's a legal question."

"In trouble again, then, is he?"

"No, it's not trouble. Not at all."

"That's what that other man said, too."

"What other man?" Sally asked, leaning forward.

"'Bout last year before Christmas, this old man come knocking just like you two, and asking for Devante. Told him exact the same as you. Don't know where he's gone to. But good riddance. Better'n having him lazin' around and me waiting on him."

"What kind of man was it who inquired?" Adam asked.

"If you mean was he like you two, yes, sort of . . . fancy. Not from around here. But also like us, I think. Mestizo."

"Did he tell you his name?"

"Yeah, but I don't remember it. Come back about another week later, looking real bad. But he was nice enough."

"And you're sure you don't know where Devante is?"

"No. Nada."

There was a pause, and Adam and Sally started to stand up.

"You want a coffee or something?" the woman said suddenly. "Don't get lot of visitors here these days. And I don't go out none."

"Well, we should go back to the office," Adam said, standing.

But Sally remained where she was and said, "We'd be happy to stay for a minute, Mrs. Sanchez. Right, Adam?"

"Of course," he said, resuming his place. "Unless you'd rather watch your novella."

"Oh, that!" the woman said, getting up slowly and starting for the kitchen. "Just about the same story every day. Lots of good-looking people always gettin' in trouble with themselves. You'd think with looks and all that money . . ."

She stood stiffly and shuffled into the kitchen.

When she was out of earshot, Adam looked at Sally with raised eyebrows. "Why did you agree to stay?" he said. "We really do need to get back to the office."

"Relax, Adam," she said. "We just barged into someone's house, disrupted her life. The least we can do is sit and chat for a minute. You do recognize loneliness, don't you? That's all it is. We're probably the most company—the most excitement she's had in weeks. And there's the mystery of why she's been visited twice with inquiries about Devante Sanchez, even if he could be the wrong person."

"OK. Yes, I get it," Adam said. "You know now why I have you around: to teach me the manners my mother forgot about."

"And I hoped it was my scintillating conversation."

"Glad you reminded me. Yes, that too."

Back in the car, heading toward the Loop against the afternoon rush-hour traffic pouring out of the city, Adam watched as they passed through a corridor of neighborhoods, warehouses, and factories. This was not a part of the city he knew well—in fact, not at all. Nor anything about the lives of the people who worked and ate and slept there, whose lives were so different from his. It was only a few miles from the office in the Loop, but a country apart, a section of Chicago that had been swept by wave after wave of immigrants. It was a vital part of the city that he would never have any reason to know with his sheltered life of contract law, club lunches, and garden parties in Winnetka.

He wondered what it had been like for Percy Landsman to search out his family in such an unfamiliar place, wondering about his mother and perhaps any siblings or descendants he might have. Their own search for Devante Sanchez had so far been just a fruitless exercise to tie up loose ends, to find out the recipients of that other will if it existed. Or at least discover what this strange man intended before his death. For them, more out of curiosity now. But for Percy, it must have been overwhelming and very personal—a quest to understand who he was after so many years of knowing only half of himself. And maybe that incomplete second will that he was contemplating had been an effort to die in his own skin.

Sally glanced briefly at him, puzzled by his silence. "Is something the matter?" she asked.

"No, not at all. I'm just thinking about Percy and what he must have been going through—searching for his family, probably knowing that he was terminally ill—and this might be the last thing he ever did. I don't know how I'd feel if I suddenly discovered something about myself that was true and essential but had been hidden for years—for almost my whole life—and obscured by the deception and lies of everyone around me. I really hope he found the solace he was looking for."

He paused and then turned to her. "It must have been strange, thinking that you could be a part of two existences: one the denial of the other. I'm no expert on adoptions, but this one has to be unusual—singular. Just think of what it meant for Percy to find out that his adopted father was actually his real father and then face the reality of his father's reluctant and deceitful acceptance. To be rejected by his father and abandoned and then picked up again like some piece of discarded litter to be recycled as his son. And to know that he had another family somewhere else, perhaps living in Chicago, perhaps someone familiar, or perhaps a person he had passed on the street or who knew about him."

"More likely driven by curiosity tinged with guilt," Sally said.

"Yes," he said. "You're probably right."

"I wonder . . ." He stopped himself because he didn't want to finish the sentence. He knew what he was about to confess to her—that his interest in Percy Landsman had deep roots in the confusion and unhappiness of his own childhood, missing the father that he never really had. He had always felt that there was something incomplete and unnatural when he was growing up—a circle half closed, a family that limped on one foot.

Of course, he could have been closer to his mother. That would have been natural. But somehow, he always considered himself an intimate stranger and that he belonged and came from somewhere else. It would be impossible to explain.

"Do you think we should try the other Devante Sanchez?" she asked.

"I suppose so. Why not? We've come this far. Might as well finish it."

"Will you be upset if we don't find him? I mean, after all this?"

"I don't know how I'll react, except that we tried, and I'm not even sure why anymore."

"Your sense of justice?"

"That's a nice way of putting it, but I'm not sure of my motivation anymore, except that something bothered me from the start—and is still bothering me. I thought I had put it to rest. But I guess I hadn't. And I don't like the feeling. On the other hand, maybe it's because you're such a pretty tenacious detective."

They drove the rest of the route in silence. Suddenly, he turned to her with a puzzled look on his face. "There's just one more thing that stumps me. That copy of a will we found. He might have drawn it up before he discovered the whereabouts of the existing family of Maria Sanchez if he did. So maybe he never actually found them, and the copy was just a preliminary sketch of something he never completed. Maybe that's all we've discovered."

"Then how did he know their names?"

"My god, of course, you're right!"

It was after six when they finally pulled into the parking garage adjacent to the office.

"I'm going to catch up on a few things," Sally said as they walked toward the exit.

"Why not have dinner with me?" Adam said. "It's the least I can do for all the driving you've done."

She stopped and put a hand on his arm, pulling him to a stop.

"Company policy," she said.

"Come on, Sally, there is no such thing. I've read the fine print. And anyway, we've had lunch together and a drink before. So why not dinner?"

"My policy then," she said. "Dinner would be a date, and I don't date a coworker."

"Is that a hard and fast rule?"

"Yep," she said, releasing his arm.

"Hard and not so fast."

He held the door that opened out onto the busy street and the uncertain light of late afternoon.

"Tomorrow, then," he said. "Maybe we can end this tomorrow. Are you up for one more interview?"

"Of course," she answered, and giving him a little shove, she disappeared into the office building.

He stood for a moment watching until the wings of the revolving door slowed and then stopped. Turning away, he walked toward the elevated train and home and a frustrating evening of wondering why it was she was so friendly and amenable at work and so elusive afterward.

The next afternoon, Sally stopped to pick him up at the exit to the parking garage.

"Ready?" she said as he buckled the seat belt.

"Yes, I'm ready for this to be over," he replied. "And you know where we're going?"

"If you mean did I put the address in the GPS, yes, I did. Otherwise?"

"Otherwise, we have no idea. Probably just the last journey in a fruitless search. But at least we're finding out more about Chicago geography," he said. *And enjoying every minute being with you*—he did not add.

Their destination was west and north of the Loop, near Logan Square, and another section of Chicago with a large Latino population. The address was a large apartment building that made the wedge of an intersection with store fronts on the first level. Luckily, there was nearby street parking, and they walked back and found the name Sanchez on the call box in a hallway off to the side.

"Maybe this is our lucky day," Sally said as she pressed the button.

Almost immediately, a voice answered in Spanish.

Adam didn't understand, but he asked for Devante Sanchez.

There was a long pause, and finally, the door lock buzzed, and they entered.

The apartment was up three flights. On their way, they passed a young man wearing a baseball cap reversed and baggy jeans, hopping down the stairs. When he saw them, he stopped with a strange, puzzled look on his face.

Sally just smiled at him, and Adam thought she could disarm almost anyone's suspicions. He also wondered what might have occurred had he been alone.

They continued up to the third floor. There were four doors on the landing, one of them open slightly.

When they approached, it opened further. A very slight girl, probably just beginning her teens and holding a cell phone, stood in the frame.

"You are looking for Devante Sanchez?" she said, making no motion to allow them to enter. "That was my grandfather. But you can't see him." She stepped back and made a motion to close the door.

"Is your mother home?" Sally asked quickly. "If we could speak to her . . ."

The girl just disappeared, and after a minute, an older woman opened the door wider. She finished wiping her hands on a dishtowel and looked carefully at Sally and Adam.

"Wasn't expecting visitors," she said, glancing down at the plain housedress she was wearing. "You're not selling anything, I hope, 'cause I'm not buying. And I'm a good Catholic if you are trying to convert me to something else. Seems like everyone's got something for you these days that you're not wanting or needing."

"We're looking for Devante Sanchez," Adam said.

"You and everyone else, it seems," the woman said.

"Could we come in and talk to you?" Sally said. "It's rather important."

"I guess you can," the woman said, back up to allow them to enter. "But I wasn't expecting visitors."

She led them into a shabby living room that was sparsely furnished: a small couch with a low table in front, an armchair, and a television set in the corner.

"Turn off that program, will you?" she said to the girl who had stationed herself cross-legged on the floor in front of it.

The girl said nothing but stood, turned off the set, and walked out of the room, turning just briefly to glare at Sally and Adam.

"If it's not the TV, it's the cell phone," the woman said. "Please sit down and tell me what you want with my father. He's not here right now."

"We're not sure that he is the actual person we're looking for," Adam said. "But maybe you can help us."

"That's what the other man asked," the woman said.

"When was that?"

"Sometime last year before Christmas. He came here looking for Devante, but I told him that my father had passed away."

"Do you remember his name?"

"Yes, of course. He left me his card. I have it in the drawer in the kitchen. I'll get it if you want, but I can tell you he asked me all sorts of questions about my family, and then he told me he was my uncle. Came back several times and then just disappeared. He was a very nice man. Brought a present for *la nina* every time he visited. Big stuffed animals and books. You could see that he didn't know what a girl nowadays wants. But he was a really nice man."

Adam looked at Sally and then at the woman. "Could you get the card he gave you?"

"Yes," she said and walked through a small nook that held a dining room table and chairs and disappeared into the kitchen.

When she returned, she handed the card to Adam. It was Percy Landsman's business card.

"And what was your grandmother's name?" Sally asked suddenly.

"Maria," the woman answered.

"And her last name before she married, do you know that?"

"Lopez. Maria Sanchez-Lopez.."

"I have to tell you, Ms. Sanchez . . ."

"Castaneda, Benita Castaneda. I was married. We moved back in with my father a couple of years ago."

"I'm afraid I have to tell you that Mr. Landsman passed away several months ago."

"I'm sorry to hear that," she said. "He promised to come back once more, but we never saw him again, and I was always thinking maybe we did something or said something. It's a sad relief to know, I guess. But I don't understand. Did you come just to tell me that?"

"I should tell you that I'm a lawyer," Adam said. "And I represent the estate of Mr. Landsman. We're just trying to locate any living relatives he might have."

"Well, I guess you have then because I'm sure he was my uncle. I saw the resemblance to my father the moment I met him. Otherwise, I would have been suspicious. It's not that I don't trust people, except maybe I don't. You can never be really sure these days."

"I don't blame you at all," Sally said. "Will Mr. Castaneda be home soon, by the way?"

"No. Sorry. He's passed. Got a terrible accident at his work and died. Didn't leave us much. But me and Julieta, we manage."

"What else did Mr. Landsman say to you, Mrs. Castaneda?" Adam asked.

The woman fidgeted for a moment, twisting her hands together as if to hold back a gesture. She looked at both of them cautiously.

"It was nothing," she began.

"But he did say something, am I right?" Sally said.

"Yes. But I'm sure he didn't mean it. Why would he?"

"But . . . ?"

"He said something about taking care of us: me and Julieta. But I didn't think nothing of it. He was just a nice man, and I guess he meant well. I think he really took to my daughter. Said he didn't have any family."

"Did he say something about a will?"

She looked puzzled for a moment. "Oh, a *testamento*, you mean? Maybe he did. Maybe not. I'm not sure."

"He did then," Sally said, "didn't he?"

"Well, yes. But it was just talk, I'm sure. You know how men can be." She stopped suddenly. "I'm very sorry. I don't know why I'm so *inhospita*. I should ask you if you want to drink something. Coffee, maybe. Something cold?"

"Please, no," Adam said. "We're fine. And just about to leave. But we'll be in touch with you. Can you write down your telephone number?" He handed her two cards. "Keep one and put your number on the back of the other."

She took the cards and studied them for a moment.

"So you are an *abogado*. And here is my number," she said after retrieving a pencil from her pocket and writing on the other card. She handed it back.

"I think we'll go then," Adam said, standing. "You'll hear from us."

"Yes," she said quietly.

"It was lovely to meet you, Mrs. Castaneda," Sally said, joining Adam at the door. "You have a pretty daughter."

Pausing outside on the doorstep of the apartment building, Sally grabbed Adam's arm.

"Did you just make a promise you can't keep?" she said. "I'm not sure she believed us."

Adam looked at her. "I'm not sure I can, but I'm certainly going to find out if Landsman actually had another will or was in the process of revising the old one. Frankly, I'm beginning to think this whole affair has the bad smell of a cover-up or worse."

"You don't think that the partners would suppress a revised will, do you? Is that what you're saying?"

"I don't know, but I certainly intend to find out. Nothing about this, from the first day, has ever seemed quite right to me."

"But why would they?"

"Do you really need me to answer that? Just look around you. Here, it's not exactly the North Side, is it?" He gestured.

"I don't understand exactly."

"People like this aren't among the deserving rich."

"You don't think much of the partners, do you, Adam? Sometimes I don't understand you at all. And you still want to become one of them? Who are you?"

"We'll see, won't we?" he said, stepping off the landing onto the sidewalk.

Driving back to the Loop, Adam glanced several times at Sally, but she refused to look back as if totally absorbed by the crowded highway. If she had turned her head, he would have asked her again to have dinner or at least a drink. It was as if she knew and wanted to signal her refusal—and save him the embarrassment of another rejection. So when she spoke, finally, she continued looking straight ahead: "Now that we've found the family, what do you plan to do?"

"I'm going to confront them upstairs," he replied. "This has gone on too long already."

"You're running a risk, aren't you? You've pretty much been warned of this already, and I know you've had your suspicion of what they might do."

"Yes, I suppose you're right about that, but what would you do?"

She slowed suddenly as a car lurched into a small space in front of them. "I suppose I'd follow my conscience."

"Lawyers don't have consciences, just clients."

"Then you need to decide who your client is in this case."

"I suppose you're right, Sally."

Chapter 10

The next morning, Adam was up early after a restless night. A sour taste lingered in his mouth from too much black coffee and a dinner he'd rather forget about. He wasn't sure when he made up his mind that evening—perhaps so gradually that he couldn't remember—but he had decided to confront the partners as soon as possible about the Landsman will . . . or wills, if there were two. He had to know and put an end to his doubts. He no longer feared what they might say or do. He had passed over those consequences long ago without really knowing it. No, what troubled him now was what he might discover about the men and a profession he had once respected. Most of all, he needed to know who he was.

Arriving at the office shortly after 8:00 a.m., he immediately called upstairs to Frank Emsback's office. His secretary answered.

"Mr. Emsback isn't in yet," she said. "I don't expect him until later this morning. Mr. Chauncey, is it? Shall I schedule an appointment?"

"Yes, please."

"How about sometime next week? Thursday looks open in the morning. I could shoehorn you into a ten o'clock slot. How will that be?"

"I'm afraid I can't wait that long," Adam replied. "I need to see him today . . . this morning if possible."

There was a moment of silence as if the secretary was anticipating the consequences of disrupting her senior's schedule.

"I'm sorry. I can't possibly do that. He's very busy today."

"All right, I understand," Adam said, putting the phone down. He knew there was no use insisting. Demands in the firm only traveled in one direction—from top to bottom. But he wondered if Emsback had left word with her to put him off. It was certainly beginning to sound like some sort of silent agreement, an evasion. And he couldn't help but imagine the worst.

He sat back in his chair and stared at the blank screen of his computer and then down at his desk. How ironic it was that at this moment, he recalled his mother's advice to think the best of everyone: the words that always made him wince even though he always half-believed them. And now he was questioning the motives of a distinguished lawyer in one of the best firms in Chicago. He had come a long way from Southern Illinois.

He opened his computer, read email, and then worked for an hour—or tried to concentrate on a brief that had been passed to him for annotation. By 10:00 a.m., he was too nervous to continue. Straightening his tie and grabbing his suit jacket hanging on the shoulders of his desk chair, he walked out of his office to the elevator bank.

Emerging into the Tower lobby, he passed by the receptionist, who gave him a puzzled look. But he just waved his hand before the man could speak and continued down the hall to Emsback's office. Knocking on the door as he opened it, he entered the room.

The secretary looked up in surprise.

"Mr. Chauncey," she said. "I thought I told you . . ."

"Yes, you did," he said, walking toward the inner office. "Is he in?"

"Yes, but . . ."

"Tell him I'm here. I'll just take a minute of his time."

"Well," she said, picking up the intercom, "Mr. Chauncey to see you, sir. I told him you were busy, but he's here anyway."

She put down the receiver and said nothing.

The door opened, and Emsback emerged, stretching out his hand.

"Come in, Adam, come in. I'm glad you're here."

Adam was sure, from the look on his face, that the senior partner was anything but pleased to see him, but he continued the charade.

"I'll just take a minute, ir. I know you're busy."

"Not at all. I'm delighted to see you. Sit down. I've been wanting to ask you something. Slipped my mind until this morning. And here you are. Sit," he said, indicating a leather arm chair at the conference table that took up the corner of the office. He chose an adjacent seat.

Folding his hands on the table, he gave Adam a quizzical look and then began: "I've been meaning to ask you . . . and some of the other partners also wanted to know: Are you interested in joining us for a round of golf?"

"Well, sir, I have played a few times, but I'm a sort of hook-and-slice guy. Not really my sport. It seems like I'm unnaturally attracted to hazards. I don't think you'd like it."

Ignoring him, Emsback continued, "Because I'd like to invite you out to the club one of these days. Some Saturday soon. With some of the partners. Make a day of it. Dinner, perhaps?"

"I appreciate that, Sir, but I'm pretty sure you'd quickly tire of someone who shoots in the hundreds and disturbs the wildlife in the woods chasing after lost balls."

Emsback laughed. "Don't underestimate yourself, Adam. False modesty. I'll bet that's another of your attributes that you've been hiding."

"Well, I can't refuse an invitation, but you've been warned."

"Fine. Good boy. I'll arrange a date. Now, if there isn't anything else, I'll let you get back to work. I'm sure they're not skimping on assignments, am I right?"

"Absolutely, sir. But, in fact, there is one more thing."

Emsback pushed back from the table and glowered at Adam.

"It's about the Landsman will."

"Damn it, son! That's a done deal. What's possibly the problem? Isn't it in probate?"

"Yes, it is, but I think that Landsman was preparing another will just before he died. We've found notes to that effect and a partial document, and what's more, we've discovered that he had another family, descended from his mother, who seemed to be new beneficiaries."

"We?"

"Well, yes, I've enlisted one of the paralegals to help me out. Entirely my doing. She's just doing some research."

Emsback stood up and walked behind his desk and sat down again. Adam was sure that this was a gesture to establish his inferiority, but he persisted anyway.

"Yes, he has a niece, and from what I can determine, he was preparing to leave her a significant part or most of his estate. I can show you the notes if you like and a copy of the tentative will."

"That proves nothing, and I don't understand why you've taken it upon yourself to become a private investigator and wasting your time and the firm's driving out with some paralegal on expeditions all over Chicago's slums."

Adam said nothing for a moment, but he was shocked that Emsback mentioned his trips with Sally. Either it was a lucky guess, or he knew something he wasn't revealing. Had they been followed? Either way, he was determined to find out.

"I'm sorry, ir, but how did you know where Landsman's relatives lived? Did you have us followed?"

"Let's just say that the firm watches over its own," Emsback shot back. And then he started to stand up. "I think you ought to leave now, Adam, for your own good, before you say something that can't be unsaid."

Adam remained seated as if the weight of the truth pressed him down in his seat. Yes, Emsback knew. He knew about the family and knew, somehow, that he and Sally had visited them. It wasn't a characteristic of his to be stubborn and confrontational or even resolute, but he suddenly felt that the firm had betrayed him and set him up because they judged him naïve and innocent. A country bumpkin from Southern Illinois who could be manipulated with a ride in a golf cart and visions of a Winnetka palace.

He decided to risk everything. "You know, don't you?" he began. "You know everything about Landsman's family history. And there's another will, isn't there? The one I sent to probate has been superseded. I'm right, aren't I?"

Emsback looked at him with the studied calm that must have impressed many a judge or litigation opponent.

"All right, Adam," he said. "Perhaps we underestimated you. And I suppose it's to your credit that you showed such initiative. Very few graduates of law school these days would have given a second thought to what was a very straightforward will. Nothing with any legal problems. No tangle to sort out and no ambiguities. I drew that will up myself, made you and Bill Evens executors, so I know. And now you've discovered something that puts the whole affair in jeopardy. I suppose I should compliment you, but of course, that's beside the point. You realize, don't you, that you've created a difficult situation? And I don't need to tell you that the partners are very unhappy about your extracurricular escapades. And don't ask me how I know, but we've kept an eye on your various travels."

"Then I'm right," Adam said. "You set me up, thinking that I would take the easy, obvious path and ignore anything that looked strange or suspicious."

"No, not at all. You're wrong. We had you co-sign as executor because it's our policy to do so, and we were worried about Bill Evans's health at the time. I would have made myself executor, except that Percy Landsman had been an acquaintance of Bill's, and he insisted on him as executor. We had no idea you'd go off on a tangent, chasing down those people. But now that you have, we need to deal with the situation you've created before it gets out of hand."

"So I'm right," Adam said. "Landsman intended to file another will."

Emsback looked at him for a long time as if he could read Adam's expression for some indication of how he should respond.

"If you must know, but I warn you, this is highly confidential," he began slowly. "You're correct about many of the details. And I'm also betting that you can be trusted to do what's right—for yourself and for the firm—when I tell you. You see, situations like this happen every once in a while, and we lawyers are called upon to make a judgment about what's necessary for the best outcome. You're young and, as you say, innocent, and you don't always see the larger picture."

He continued, "Lawyers have to serve their clients, but every once in a while, we have to step in and overrule some fantasy or whim that will lead to a terrible outcome. They don't teach you about that in law school, of course. Yes, I can see that you're surprised. But the law isn't just about following rules and regulations. It's ultimately about achieving justice—the just conclusion that is in everyone's best interest. And I dare say, society's as well."

He stopped for a moment and smiled at Adam in a way that looked to Adam like a threat. "And in this case," he continued, "in Percy Landsman's case, it means fulfilling his original bequests, his real intention. Whatever he may have subsequently thought was a pipedream, some sort of childish fantasy. The kind of sentiment that might come over you when you think you're about to die. Damn, how many times we've had to confront such a situation! Anyway, perhaps Landsman felt he hadn't lived a perfect life, and he wanted to make amends. Or maybe he was just senile. But in any event—you do understand that, don't you?—we have to honor his best wishes, not his whims."

Adam realized he was taking a chance, but he had to know. "So there's another will, isn't there? Those notes we found . . . And he as much as told his niece that he was going to put her in his will. I'm right, aren't I?"

"I'm going to tell you, Adam, something about yourself. You see, we took a chance on you," Emsback said. "It was our little experiment in democracy. Although I have to confess I had my doubts about you—serious doubts, if you have to know—that you would ever make partner. Wrong school, wrong background. I could see immediately that you weren't one of us. To tell you the truth, I opposed hiring you and voted against it. But you impressed everyone else, so we decided to take a chance. Thought that ambition would cancel out all your social shortcomings. It can sometimes do a lot to make up for an unsuitable pedigree. But now, here you are in my office. Are you trying to prove me right?"

"So there is another will. And signed! It's true, isn't it?" Adam insisted.

Emsback glared at him. "Yes, yes, of course. You guessed right. Landsman wrote another will, had it witnessed right here in the office, and it's entirely valid. I tried to talk him out of it, but he was so stubborn, and it's hard to argue with a dying man. But I'm certain that it wasn't what he really wanted. Just the giddy ravings of a silly old man who, on his deathbed, tries to right all the wrongs of the world. It happens far too often. And then I told him we'd end up in court anyway because such a will is sure to be contested by the rightful heirs."

"And so you decided what was best? That most of his estate should go to his brother and just ignore the existence of his other family?"

"If you want to put it that way, I suppose so, yes."

"And you suppressed that will for that reason?"

"Not entirely. You see, he dictated it and signed it, but he was clearly not in a stable condition mentally to do so. That's why the prior document is preferable."

"And you're quite sure of that? Despite the fact that you are doing something illegal?" Adam interrupted, realizing that he was cross-examining a man who was himself judging every question he asked. But once down this path, he couldn't stop; he needed to go through to the end, whatever the consequences.

Emsback laughed suddenly, but there was nothing like merriment in his voice.

"You think rather highly of your opinions, don't you, young man? I suppose it's wonderful to be young and headstrong and utterly confident in your beliefs. Well, let me tell you why you're wrong, absolutely wrong. And, if you wish to continue with the firm, you'll need to understand a few basic facts of life. You see, giving money to people like that—people of that kind—is just throwing coins in a fountain and thinking that all your dreams will automatically come true. But I'm sure you're aware of what happens when ordinary people, poor people, suddenly happen upon large sums of money. Over and over again, and it occurs to winners of the lottery, professional athletes, prize fighters, movie stars, gamblers—it overwhelms them. It makes them rich momentarily, but they always end up poor, usually in debt, because they don't understand and cherish money for the good it can do. They give it away to their friends. They buy yachts and fancy houses and cars. King for a day and then pauper for the rest of their lives. Or maybe they'll just buy drugs and spend their lives in a stupor. You know, don't you? It would overwhelm them, completely disrupt their lives. What a waste it would be to give part of Landsman's estate to people who have no responsibility and no culture. No, money should remain in the hands of those who know what to do with it, who will treat it carefully, lovingly, and make prudent investments that will not just enrich themselves but society as a whole."

"That sounds like some weird capitalist proverb: 'And the rich shall inherit the earth,'" Adam said.

Emsback was silent for a moment, studying the young man who sat across from his desk.

"No," he replied, "on the contrary, it's the golden rule of common sense."

"Don't you think . . ."

"No, emphatically, no! I do not think anything!" Emsback said, holding up his hand as if to intercept Adam's words in mid-air. "Enough of this nonsense! If you wish to continue with the firm, in any capacity, you'll give up this fantasy immediately and realize what's best for everyone concerned, including Percy Landsman's Latino relatives. Don't destroy their lives and yours by embarking on some self-righteous crusade. Leave it alone and get on with your work, your life's work, and your career."

Adam was silent for a moment, stunned by the anger in Emsback's voice.

"You can still be one of us, Adam," he said, softening suddenly. "You should realize what you signed on for. The side you're on."

"I'm sorry, sir. I didn't realize there were 'sides,' as you put it. I stand corrected."

Emsback stood up and waved his hand toward the door.

"This meeting is over now. You need to think carefully about whether you want a future in this firm." He paused as Adam stood and walked toward the exit and then resumed: "I admire someone who can hold their own with me, son. It's rare enough that one of the juniors has the fortitude to answer back. It'll serve you well in the profession if you remain. But the same strength can harden into obstinacy and self-righteousness, and it'll destroy you. I would be very careful of what you do."

"Thank you, sir," Adam said, pausing as he walked out. "I'll take that as a warning."

Adam stood mute outside the closed door to the office, looking down the hallway with its thick tread and hushed ambiance. A place here would come at a substantial cost if it came at all—hard work, endless billable hours, compromise. He wondered if it was worth it. Walking on, he could feel a damp sweat crawl across his chest and under his arms. It was as if his body was telling him what his mind was trying to deny. He had to admit that he was shocked by the tone he had taken with Emsback that roused the latter's anger. It wasn't bravery on his part, he thought, just a flash of irritation and resentment—the troublesome underside of impatience and ambition. He wondered if, in some way, he was jealous of the older man, envying his curated demeanor, his position in the firm, his elegant office, his smooth life, his self-confidence. *Is that what it was, though?* he wondered. *Or was it something else? Not envy at all, but disgust.*

Back downstairs, his first thought was to call Sally—to confide in her, hoping that she would approve of his harsh exchange with Emsback. Instead, he just sat at his desk, mulling over what he should do next. It would be wrong to involve her anymore. He had been given a clear choice: his career or what? Some legal maneuver to pry the second will out of wherever Emsback had stowed it. He would certainly lose everything now: his job, his apartment, perhaps even risk disbarment. He wouldn't put it past the upstairs lawyers to shoot at him with every legal strategy they could think of and tie him up in court appearances and lawsuits ranging from the obscure to the frivolous. But he then wondered if it would come to that. He could imagine the damage done if the firm was accused of suppressing a perfectly legal will. The legal scribes would love to bring down that elephant. Of course, the partners might find a way to prevent the terrible publicity. In the end, he might even face some criminal charge.

No, he thought, *not likely. I'm holding a dangerous trump card that would bring about a catastrophic deluge of bad publicity for the firm—if I choose to play it. But at the same time, it's too hot to keep in my vest pocket if I choose not to. Either way will be a disaster. I've created that for myself.*

He wondered—except that he knew now—even if he let the whole issue hide in some dusty file drawer, they would never trust him upstairs. No doubt in the future, while he languished here at the bottom of the hierarchy of juniors, charged with the most boring contract work, he would finally realize that he would never take that last elevator ride up to a partnership. He would remain nothing but an overpaid paralegal for the rest of his career. And if he told Landsman's other family about the will, he would be fired immediately. The firm would have no difficulty finding some sort of excuse to do so. Either way, he knew he had sacrificed himself—not out of principle—but from a fatal curiosity. Or maybe there was a fraction of integrity in his motivation. He had never been very good at self-examination, never really sure of himself, and he had no idea how to begin. Maybe Sally could help him after all.

He didn't need to reach out to her because, shortly before lunch, she knocked at his door. He couldn't help noticing how fresh and professional she looked today. It was one of the things he enjoyed most about her: her ever-changing moods reflected in the outfits she chose. Today, she had a tailored blue suit with a white blouse and a dark-colored bow, knotted like a short tie at the throat. All business.

"Sit down," he said, a bit too brusquely. "I've got something to tell you. And don't interrupt until I finish."

She looked at him curiously but chose the chair in front of his desk.

"Sorry for my tone of voice," he began. "But you'll see pretty quickly why I'm upset."

She said nothing.

"I just got back from upstairs. Short interview—if you want to call it that—with Frank Emsback about the two Landsman wills." He watched her face darken. "Yes, you might have guessed it would come to that, I'm supposing. Anyway, I'm afraid I was pretty blunt with him, and I really don't know why. Something about the setting—that office with its posh furnishings and thick carpet. I don't know why it made me so nervous. Or just angry seeing him so confident—self-satisfied and smug. But I told him that I—and I kept you out of it—had located Landsman's other family. Strangely enough, he seemed to know all about it and our research. And then I asked him if Landsman had made another will and signed it, and he admitted it. Just like that. Without a hesitation. I don't know what he expected from me—most likely that I would agree with him and affirm his crackpot sociology that it was wiser to let Landsman's brother inherit the lot. He read me some sort of sermon that being wealthy and well-bred and distinguished made the brother more deserving than the Latino family.

"I guess he could read on my face or interpret my objections that I thought it was unjust to suppress a perfectly valid will for the sake of some theory about how poor people can't handle money—or don't deserve it. When he realized that I wouldn't play along, he threatened me. Not of course with violence. It was all fist in a velvet glove. That's never his style.

But it amounts to the same. And I'm afraid I'm through here. No, I'm certain I'm finished. Whatever I do, they will never trust me again. How could they? Might keep me on if I don't say anything. Maybe even pay me well. You know, keep your enemy close to hand and well fed and quiet! But I'm sure I'm through. And if I try to reveal the other will, I'll be gone in an instant before you can say, 'Dismissed with prejudice.' I'm afraid I've fucked up my legal career forever. Who would hire a young attorney fired for cause?"

Sally straightened in her chair when he finished. "Are you feeling sorry for yourself now? Sounds like it."

"No, I don't think so. Just being realistic about my prospects."

"Good. Because I think you've done something admirable."

"Really? But awfully foolhardy. I can't even remember back to when we started this investigation. Why I was so keen to do it."

"But you did. And I helped you. I'm partly to blame. I urged you on."

"No. You only did what I asked you to. You could hardly refuse. I don't think that the firm will blame you. In fact, I'll make sure they don't. I can always say I brought you along to be a silent witness. Implicated you despite your objections."

"Except that I chauffeured you all over Chicago."

"Fine. That just makes you the firm's Uber driver. Nothing more. No, you're out of it, Sally."

"I wouldn't mind, you know."

"Yes. But I refuse to let you be dragged down with me."

"So what have you decided to do?"

"I haven't decided exactly."

"I think you have," she said. "I think you knew all along that something was amiss. You're really innocent and maybe a bit screwed up, Adam, if I might say so. But eventually, you do the right thing."

"I suppose I didn't think it out—all the implications."

"I'm glad you didn't. Didn't allow some sort of loyalty to the upstairs make you lose your moral bearings. You did the right thing."

"But look at the consequences."

"I'm staring right at them, and I think what I see is someone who never wanted to make partner in the first place, someone who didn't want to pay such high dues to have an elegant office and a club membership. You were never like them, Adam. Admit it. You thought you were, but you weren't."

"But maybe I could have been. It's what I thought I wanted all along."

"Just to prove yourself to an audience that you'd come to despise? What's the joy in that?"

Adam was quiet for a moment, trying not to stare at this remarkable woman sitting across from him.

"I'm afraid you know me too well, Sally—better than myself."

"Only because you're pretty transparent even with all your hesitations."

"Well, I never saw it."

"Who can really know themselves: too much history and self-deception. Too many contradictions. It's like trying to find your true self in a mirror when all you can see is the reverse image of the person you think you are. Never the way others see you."

"I'm sure you're right, Sally. I've acted without thinking, and now I have to make the most important decision in my life, unless it's already been made for me!"

"My only advice: just don't be hasty," she said, standing up and walking toward the door. "But I'm sure you'll do what's best."

When she left, it seemed to him that the room was suddenly vacant, empty of all personality, and utterly without character. He wondered why he had never bothered to put pictures on the walls or framed his diploma in something more than cheap, dull wood. And the lone window was just a gray rectangle of Chicago sky—nothing here to make it his own. Did that mean something? Why had he neglected to bring anything personal: photographs, even some art object, a bookshelf. He had just moved into this space without ever owning it. Did it mean he was counting on a hasty promotion? So why bother if this was just a temporary transit? Or was he reluctant to be here at all? Had something held him back from committing himself to the firm all along? He had no idea. And it was far too late to begin understanding that now.

He leaned back in his chair, looking intently—but without really seeing—at the blank window, letting his eyes relax their focus to a blur. It was rare that he nodded off during the day, but this morning, he felt a strange fatigue, an overpowering exhaustion. He was unaware of dozing off until his head jerked back painfully. Or maybe it was a loud knock at the door that roused him.

He stood up, stretched, and walked over to open it.

"I almost thought you weren't here, Adam," Frank Emsback said, stepping into the office. "I had to knock twice."

"Sorry, Sir. I guess I was distracted."

"Let's sit for just a moment." He settled into a chair at the conference table and then slid a manila file across to Adam who had come over to join him.

"You'll see it's the second Landsman will," he began. "Read it over carefully because I want you to see how troubled his mind had become when he made these strange bequests. He couldn't possibly know that other family, told me that he had just discovered their existence, and then he went completely overboard and left them almost all of his estate, cutting his own brother out almost entirely. I'm sure you'll agree that this document reflects the sudden impulse of a whimsical mind, distracted by the fear of dying. Or maybe feeling some sudden affection for people he thought he was obliged to cherish. I have no idea what it's like to be an adopted son and then suddenly find your birth mother and your biological family. But it goes to show you how such a discovery can inspire dangerous thoughts of guilt and anger and atonement. Personally, I've always thought it a bad idea to break the seal of adoption.

"And, I'm no psychologist," he continued carefully, "but you'll understand when I tell you that I have considerable experience with writing wills, and I assure you it's often a perilous moment to think of shuffling off everything that you own, dividing up the accumulations of a lifetime. How many times have I persuaded a client not to try to rearrange someone's life with a bequest: to right some wrong or maybe even seek revenge from the grave? A will is your only brief with immortality, and you have to be careful how you compose it."

He started to get up, putting both hands on the table for balance: "You'll see that you are still listed as the second executor, although you never signed it. So let me know what you decide to do. I'm sure you'll choose what's best for you and the firm and for Landsman's memory and keep quiet about it."

"And if I choose to reveal this will, how can you explain its sudden appearance?"

"That wouldn't be a problem, of course. You see, Bill Evans is the first executor, and you know his memory problems. Just didn't remember to keep a copy. And the witness was one of our secretaries. And we had to let her go several months ago. And I've been on vacation until recently. And we couldn't contact you to sign. So we can say that no one knew about it, and we just recently discovered the original document among Landsman's possessions. No one will ask any questions—that is until the will is challenged. And then I doubt very much it will hold up in court. I'm sure we'll be able to break it. We'll certainly try!"

Emsback stood up abruptly and walked over to the door. Looking around the room, he said, "You know, Adam, you ought to do something about this office. Make it more personal. Make it a cheerful place. That is if you intend to stay with us." And he left, closing the door behind him.

Adam remained seated with the pages of the will spread out in front of him. Emsback certainly had made a valid argument; it was indeed possible that Landsman was distracted when he dictated his last testament. And Landsman's brother would certainly have grounds to contest it. But it was illegal—obviously and patently illegal—to suppress this second will, whatever the possible reasons to do so. If it came to a court case, it would be up to the judge to determine which will to honor. And he could see arguments for both, although he was pretty sure this would stand.

But what bothered him most was the willingness of the partners to suppress a perfectly valid document, as if they were preemptive judge and jury. He knew he had no choice. He would insist that the second will be filed with the county court, and he would inform the family of its contents. Nor did he have any illusions about his future at Smithson and Dwyer either. He would immediately lose even this dingy first-floor office—and perhaps any chance at a partnership anywhere in Chicago—once his disloyalty to the partners made the rounds of the downtown clubs, golf courses, cocktail parties, and preferred watering holes where the senior members of the profession hung out to exchange the latest gossip.

There was one more decision he had to make that had far more serious consequences for the firm and himself. Should he report the intentional suppression of the latest will? It made him furious—he had to admit that now—to think what Emsback had done: what it signaled about the firm and, by implication, himself. It was nothing but a conspiracy of wealth and position. However, if he made an issue of it, that might complicate the just outcome he wanted for Landsman's family and tie things up in court for years. And he wanted the family to receive its due more than some potential chastisement of his superiors. He would not let them have their conspiracy; he would allow the partners their fiction about how the second will had been overlooked. But he would not allow them to assign him any blame. He knew too much for that. This was a perfect definition of a stymy—a duel of two sides, each armed with a devastating weapon, in which the first shot would ironically kill the shooter.

It was the middle of the afternoon before he became conscious of the time and the decision he had made. He picked up the phone and called Frank Emsback's office.

He thought he could hear an anxious catch in the senior lawyer's voice when he replied, "You've come to a decision then, have you, Chauncey? I'm sure it's the right one."

"Yes, I'm sure it is too, sir," he replied. "I think we have no choice but to file the second will, whatever the consequences."

There was silence at the other end for a moment.

"Yes, there will be consequences. We'll have to contest it, of course. It's not right. Landsman clearly wasn't thinking straight. Are you sure you want to jeopardize everything?"

"And one more thing," Adam interrupted. "I have no intention of suggesting to anyone that the firm purposely suppressed the second will, but I'll insist that it be substituted for the earlier document. Maybe challenge Bill Evans as executor and have the court appoint someone. I'm not sure I should stay on as second."

"I'm not so sure that will work," Emsback replied quickly. "It seems that Bill Evans has made a complete recovery. So he will be the executor."

"That's no problem then. I'm certain he can explain everything to the court."

"Perhaps."

"Of course, he will. As I said before, I won't be making any accusations unless, of course, the will isn't filed."

Emsback hung up abruptly, but Adam knew that he had understood the threat.

He sat quietly for a moment, and then he thought: what was the name of that lawyer he met in the bar? Rachael something—no, it was Rebecca. He was sure he had her card somewhere, so he pulled out the center drawer of his desk. Rummaging through the papers and odd pens, he found what he was looking for: the card from Rebecca at Morgan and West. Perfect. The Sanchez family would need a good lawyer, someone hungry for a fight, as he remembered his impression of her.

Then leaning forward, he moved the mouse of his desktop to compose a letter.

To the Partners of Smithson and Dwyer:

This letter is to inform you that as of today, April 25, I am tendering my resignation from the law firm of Smithson and Dwyer. I deeply appreciate the opportunities that you have offered me, but circumstances make it impossible for me to continue my employment.

Sincerely yours,

Adam Chauncey

As he was printing it out, there was a knock on his door. He walked over to open it. Rachael Underwood from Human Relations was standing in the hallway.

Without being invited to do so, she swept quickly into the office as if to claim possession of it. Of course, Adam knew the purpose of her errand.

"I guess you beat me to it," he said. "I was just printing out my letter of resignation."

"That's fine, sir," she said, "We always appreciate cooperation."

Adam could almost see her relax.

"You'll need to take your things and be gone by the end of the day," she said, regaining her stiffness. "If you don't mind, I'll put a freeze on your computer and email account. Just as a precaution, of course. And I'll need your keys."

Saying this, she walked over to his desk and sat down in his chair. After she had typed something, she unplugged the computer.

"You won't be able to use this again or access any company records or your email account. Please leave anything that belongs to the firm here. Take only what's yours."

"I'm afraid that's not very much," he said. "But, of course, I understand."

She stood up and started to walk out.

"Do you like doing this?" he asked.

She turned around and looked at him intently as if measuring her words.

"It's a job."

"I suppose it keeps the partners' hands unsullied. Trouble just vanishes out of their sight. Like a crime with a hired gun and with plausible deniability. Gives them an alibi."

She walked back to the door and paused for a moment.

"No hard feelings," he said.

"That's for the best," she replied and left.

He walked over to the printer and picked up the resignation letter. He signed it quickly, placed it in an envelope, and then left the office. Taking the elevator up to the reception area, he approached the desk where the young man was deeply engrossed in reading something on his cell phone. When he finally looked up, Adam handed him the letter:

"I think this ought to go to Frank Emsback," he said.

The man smiled at him and nodded, and Adam suspected he already knew that he had been terminated. Bad news had a higher velocity than anything good ever did, and he was sure that his fate was known to almost everyone by now. He retreated quickly and rode the elevator back down to his office for the last time.

He picked up the box that Underwood had left him and emptied his meager possessions into it. Looking around, he was almost relieved that there were no pictures on the wall or photographs anywhere, just his law school diploma, which he also placed in the box. The only file he took was the Landsman will. He wasn't sure he had a right to keep it, but he fully intended to inform the Latino family of its contents, even if he couldn't show it to them.

As he was preparing to leave, Sally marched in without being invited.

"Damn you, Adam," she said. "Damn you! I never expected . . ."

"So you've heard. I was expecting a little more sympathy. It's not every day that I get fired."

"Why did you have to make a martyr of yourself?"

"I didn't . . . not purposely. I'm not good at self-analysis. That's not one of my traits. I assure you."

"Wasn't there some way to compromise, something that wouldn't end up this way?"

"No, I don't think so, Sally. And maybe I just wanted this as an excuse to quit. I'm not sure that I ever belonged here, except that I'm certain now. It was the right thing to do."

"I'm going to miss you."

"You don't need to."

She walked over to the conference table and sat down.

When she saw his confusion, she said, "Sit down, won't you! You don't have to leave quite yet, and I have something to tell you."

"All right," he said, taking a place opposite her.

"Let's drop the discussion of wills or partnerships for just a minute."

"Suits me fine."

"Good. Then I'll answer that question you asked me."

"What question?" he said. "Am I missing something?"

She grabbed his hand across the table. "I'd gladly have dinner and drinks with you."

"But I thought you wouldn't . . . date someone in the firm."

"But you're not here anymore, are you?"

"I suppose once I walk out that door, I'm not."

"Then I'd love to go out with you."

Adam laughed at the irony. "Now I have another question: Did you set me up by encouraging me to find Landsman's other family? Was driving all over Chicago just some plan of yours?"

Sally withdrew her hands and smiled. "You must think rather highly of yourself, Adam, to imagine I'd do something like that. No, I was just trying to follow my own rules, the ones I invented to stay sane at work: do what's asked of you and don't become involved with anyone."

"Then let's go," he said, standing up and grabbing the box with his few belongings. "You can escort me out of the building, and once we're on the street, I'll ask you again if you'll have dinner with me."

"And I'll say yes again."

About the Author

James Gilbert

After an academic career during which he authored ten works on modern American History, (one of them a *New York Times* notable book), James Gilbert turned to fiction. He has now written a book of short stories and five novels, three of them a mystery series set in Puerto Vallarta, Mexico.

The Legacy is his sixth published work.

He has twice won awards from the annual F. Scott Fitzgerald short story contest.

Born in Chicago, he grew up in a small suburb just to the south of the city. He graduated from Carleton College in Minnesota and earned a doctoral degree in history at the University of Wisconsin. While a professor at the University of Maryland, he taught at several universities in Europe and Australia as a visiting professor. He currently resides in Silver Spring, Maryland.

www.ingramcontent.com/pod-product-compliance
Lightning Source LLC
Chambersburg PA
CBHW031418200726
48285CB00017BA/2431